MOHANASWAMY

Praise for *Mohanaswamy*

'Much like the great James Baldwin, the acclaimed Kannada writer Vasudhendra has transformed his personal experience of bigotry, shame and tragedy into harrowing but magnificent truth-telling. His work will leave you impatient with other writers.'

– Siddharth Dube, author of *No One Else*

'Vasudhendra's stories are as real as can be. Upon reading, they become your stories, or your neighbours' or of someone you know. Mohanaswamy touched my heart. I was unaware of his world, his fears and his dreams. A book of its own kind.'

– Sudha Murty, chairperson of *Infosys Foundation*

'Vasudhendra is among the most popular writers in the contemporary Kannada scene. His collection of gay stories – a pioneering effort – has not only caused a stir in the Kannada literary world, but has also opened the reader to relationships that so far formed the underbelly of society. The love, lust, separation, power and pangs of this man to man world is shocking, even as it exposes us to a body politics that is starkly different from what operates in a man to woman relationship. The very act of writing these stories is daring, and Vasudhendra, in the true sense is a writer-activist.'

– Vivek Shanbhag, author of *Ghachar Ghochar*

'Vasudhendra's stories are moist with pain. They are simple. Their simplicity shines when you read them. Almost folkloric and far away from modern compulsions and conventions of the plot. You begin to trust that it all happened. And fearfully, you trust that it's still going on.'

– Sachin Kundalkar, author of *Cobalt Blue*

MOHANASWAMY

VASUDHENDRA

Translated from the Kannada by
Rashmi Terdal

HARPERPERENNIAL

First published in India in 2016 by Harper Perennial
An imprint of HarperCollins *Publishers*
A-75, Sector 57, Noida, Uttar Pradesh 201301, India
www.harpercollins.co.in

First published in Kannada by Chanda Pustaka, 2013

This edition published in India in 2019 by Harper Perennial

2 4 6 8 10 9 7 5 3 1

'Bed Bug' was first published in *Out of Print magazine*

P-ISBN: 978-93-5302-491-8
E-ISBN: 978-93-5302-660-8

Typeset in 12/16 Adobe Caslon Pro by
Jojy Philip, New Delhi

Printed and bound at
Thomson Press (India) Ltd

For

Mohanaswamy and his friends

Mohanaswamy's father, grandfather and great-grandfather

Mohanaswamy's son, grandson and great-grandson

CONTENTS

THE GORDIAN KNOT

The evening glow had faded into darkness, but the lights had not yet been switched on in the house. Although Mohanaswamy had come back from office at 5.30 p.m. as usual, he was not his usual self. He went straight to the puja room and squatted down in front of the idol of Lord Krishna. Restless and overwrought, he fixed his eyes on Krishna and engaged in a silent conversation with him while the Lord stood still in his wooden frame, with the flute at his lips and the familiar bewitching smile on his face.

Normally, after coming back from office, Mohanaswamy would switch on the radio. He would keep the pressure cooker on the stove and sweep the floors clean, eagerly awaiting Karthik's arrival. 'Where are you?' he would send him an SMS and wait impatiently for the mobile phone to beep with a reply.

But today he was not in a mood to do any of that. Forlorn and heartbroken, he sat in front of Krishna for what seemed like hours, with his eyes closed.

On his way back home, he had bought half a kilo of ladies' fingers from the market. Ladies' finger curry, shallow-fried in oil and liberally sprinkled with chilli powder, was Karthik's favourite. He savoured every bite of it. 'You cook better than my mother,' he would exclaim to Mohanaswamy, whose heart swelled with happiness.

Today also Mohanaswamy had planned to surprise Karthik by rustling up his favourite dish. But as soon as he reached home, Shobha aunty, Karthik's distant relative, had called. Her husband worked for a reputed company in Bengaluru. They owned a big house at Vijayanagar. Karthik and Mohanaswamy lived in Malleshwaram. The couple knew Mohanaswamy well as he had accompanied Karthik to their house several times. During one of their visits, Mohanaswamy had given them some chatnipudi which he had prepared. Shobha aunty's husband loved it so much that he pestered her to call Mohanaswamy and take down the recipe. This hadn't gone down well with Shobha aunty, who found it ridiculous to call up a twenty-five-year-old man and ask for cooking advice.

But she could not disobey her husband. So she called Mohanaswamy reluctantly.

Mohanaswamy knew that Shobha aunty was scared stiff of her husband. One evening, he had gone to her house alone to give her something. The main door was wide open, but the lights were out. 'Aunty…' he called out as he fumbled into the dining hall. There she was, sitting at the dining table, sobbing her heart out. Bemused, Mohanaswamy went near her. Seeing him, she began weeping aloud.

'What happened, Aunty?' he asked in concern.

'That bolimaga, the son a shaved widow, twisted my arm so badly. I can't take the pain!' she said, showing her right hand.

Then she began massaging her hurt arm gently with her left hand, smearing some oil on it. It took a while for Mohanaswamy to figure out whom she was referring to. On realizing that the 'bolimaga' was none other than her husband, he felt sad.

'But why did he do that, Aunty?' he asked in a low voice, softly touching her hand.

'Aaah…!' she withdrew her hand, screaming in pain. 'He comes to me only when he wants my body. He doesn't even care about my likes and dislikes in bed,' she said harshly, spewing venom. Mohanaswamy sat with her for a while before returning home. He did not mention this to Karthik. The next time he met Shobha aunty, she seemed normal and spoke to him cheerfully, as if nothing had happened. Mohanaswamy felt relieved. However, the image of Shobha aunty sitting in darkness and massaging her hand loomed before his eyes frequently.

Today, after briefly explaining the chatnipudi recipe over the phone, Mohanaswamy got into a casual conversation. 'So, how's life, Aunty? What's happening?' he asked.

'Everything's fine, Mohana. As you know, we all have to pack and be ready for our Mumbai trip next week,' she said effusively.

Mohanaswamy was bewildered. She had mentioned 'we all' and that confused him. He wasn't sure whether he was included in this. 'To Mumbai? Why, Aunty?' he asked hesitantly.

'You are asking me? Why, did your friend Karthik not tell you? Next week he is getting engaged! The ceremony is in Mumbai! How come you didn't know about it?' she said in a surprised tone.

Mohanaswamy's world came crashing down. Was Karthik really getting engaged? 'I don't know, Aunty, Karthi did not tell me,' he spoke with a choked voice, trying hard to compose himself.

'Oh … he didn't tell you? Perhaps he wanted to give

you a surprise. He saw the girl four weeks ago and agreed to marry her. He has seen quite a few girls before, but hadn't liked any of them. But this girl, she is so pretty, he said "yes" to her in the blink of an eye. She is very beautiful, has big wide eyes. And stylish too, becoming of a Mumbai girl. They speak Kannada at home. Her father is from Dharwad. But our Karthi – born and brought up in a village – has seen city life only recently. He is completely besotted with her. I worry that once they get married, she may twist him around her little finger. Anyway, they say that marriages are made in heaven, so we don't really know who's made for whom,' she said with a sigh, finally ending her long speech.

Mohanaswamy feared he would end up weeping if he spoke further. He disconnected the phone immediately and texted her: 'Aunty, signal is weak'. He switched off the mobile, threw it in a corner and then sat in front of the Krishna idol, shivering and crying.

It slowly began to dawn upon him why Karthik had become so secretive of late. He would stealthily step out of the house to make calls. He would even take his cellphone to the bathroom sometimes. When he came home late, he gave lame excuses about being caught up with work. Mohanaswamy had not suspected anything out of the ordinary. Now, as the truth behind his strange behaviour flashed across Mohanaswamy's mind, he sat in utter disbelief. The tender ladies' fingers that he had brought for Karthik lay forgotten on the floor in a corner.

The doorbell rang at 8.30 p.m. and Mohanaswamy felt somewhat relieved. It must be Karthik. 'I know you will never deceive me, I know,' he whispered into Krishna's ears as he took the idol in his hand and kissed it passionately. Karthik rang the bell incessantly. Though he had a set of keys with him, he never carried them to office. Unlike Mohanaswamy, he didn't believe in discipline. Real happiness lay in acting as per the need of the hour. But Mohanaswamy's disposition was quite different. He would lose his peace of mind for the whole day if he put a little extra salt in the curry by mistake. For him, everything in the house should be in order. The bed should always be clean, without a single crease on the sheet. The bathroom should be spick and span, else he would lose a night's sleep over it. Trousers, shirts and other clothes shouldn't be seen hanging here and there. He promptly washed his and Karthik's clothes, ironed them neatly and kept them in their place.

As the doorbell continued to ring, Mohanaswamy switched on the lights and opened the door. The sight of Karthik at the door was somewhat reassuring. I am unnecessarily worried. Nothing of that sort has happened, Mohanaswamy thought firmly. As was their routine, he took the helmet from Karthik's hands and kept it in a corner. 'Why are you so late, Karthi?' he asked him affectionately.

'So much work in the office, Mohana...' Karthik mumbled, sitting on a chair and removing his shoes.

'Don't lie,' Mohanaswamy said as he went near Karthik and pulled his head close to his chest, running fingers through his thick hair.

Karthik did not know what to say and rubbed his nose against Mohanaswamy's chest, pulling him even closer.

Caressing his cheeks, ears and back, Mohanaswamy said, 'Shobha aunty had called. Tell me, is it true?' Karthik continued rubbing his nose. 'Tell me, Karthi, please. I won't feel bad,' he insisted.

'Yes...' uttered Karthik, the sound coming from deep within his throat.

Mohanaswamy listened aghast as his worst fears came true. Pushing Karthik away, he sank against the wall, sobbing.

Karthik went near him and began wiping his tears. 'Don't cry, Mohana, please don't cry. I can't bear to see you cry.'

Mohanaswamy cried uncontrollably. 'Tell me what can I do? How long can I live like this? Should I not get married? Tell me,' Karthik asked him in a soft voice, taking him in his arms.

A deep silence reigned for a few minutes, interrupted only by Mohanaswamy's sobs.

After some time, Mohanaswamy broke the silence. 'Karthi, let's go to the mess and have dinner. I didn't cook today. I had got ladies' fingers to make curry for you but was in no mood to cook,' he said. That settled the matter somewhat.

'It's okay, you can make the curry tomorrow. Now come on, chin up! Let's go to the mess and eat. But make it fast, I'm famished,' Karthik said with alacrity as he walked to the bathroom.

Mohanaswamy opened the wardrobe, took out a clean towel and spread it across the steel rod in the bathroom. 'I have kept a towel for you,' he screamed.

'Okay, okay,' shouted Karthik, rubbing his face with soap.

'Say thanks,' cried Mohanaswamy.

'Thank you, sweetheart,' Karthik said.

~

The mess was bursting at the seams. They had to wait for a long time to get a table. By the time they got back home, it was past ten. Usually when they went out on the bike, Mohanaswamy, riding pillion, hugged Karthik tightly from behind, holding him by the waist with his left hand and placing his right hand on his thigh. Karthik was a rash rider, but that did not perturb Mohanaswamy who sat comfortably, leaning his head against his back, with his eyes closed. When they stopped at signals, Karthik slowly caressed his hand. The touch made the hair on Mohanaswamy's skin rise.

But today, nothing of that sort happened. Mohanaswamy had decided not to touch Karthik. Why hold on to the relationship with a man who, in a few months, will leave him for another person? He shrank away from his touch and sat holding the rear handle of the bike, even as Karthik tried to move backwards in a bid to touch his thighs on the pretext of adjusting his posture. When they stopped at a signal, Karthik took Mohanaswamy's hand, but Mohanaswamy pulled back instantly.

'What a mess,' Karthik had attempted a pun upon seeing people milling in and out of the mess. Mohanaswamy kept a straight face. However, amid this tense air, there was a moment of relief. Karthik had choked on an especially spicy sambar and was coughing heavily. There was no water on the table and a panicked Mohanaswamy got up quickly from his seat, went across to another table and got a glass of water. He kept looking at Karthik's face anxiously and felt relieved only after Karthik drank the water and stopped coughing. 'Are you okay now? Do you feel better?' Mohanaswamy asked.

Karthik did not speak but looked at Mohanaswamy with a smile on his face and a twinkle in his eyes.

Even after returning home, he did not allow Karthik to touch him. Karthik went off to sleep as soon as they got into the bed and began snoring softly. But sleep evaded Mohanaswamy. I took out all my frustrations on Karthi for no reason. Poor thing! What can he do if his parents force him to get married? Isn't it cruel on my part to stop him for my own selfish reasons? My Karthi deserves hundred such beautiful women. How can I bridle his youthfulness? Such thoughts baffled Mohanaswamy as he lay next to Karthik, tossing and turning.

Karthik may spread his arms towards me any moment. If he does, I will not refuse, Mohanaswamy said to himself, wistfully. He kept staring at Karthik through the darkness. If my love for him is true, he will wake up within a minute and look at me, he thought. He waited impatiently, counting from one to hundred. He prayed to Krishna as well. But Karthik didn't wake up even after ten minutes. In fact, his snoring reached a new high.

Finally a hapless Mohanaswamy decided to break his resolve. Defeat wasn't new to him after all. He knew by experience that he could not afford to insist on winning. He slowly inched towards Karthik. Grabbing him gently, Mohanaswamy began rubbing his nose behind Karthik's ear. Karthik woke up at his touch.

Mohanaswamy trembled at this sudden rage. He felt jilted. Is he the same Karthik who used to feel aroused just by reading my text messages? And now, even my naked body is not enough. My Karthi – who used to pester me for sex all night – has now gone off to sleep in another room. 'Mohana…' he used to call me sweetly, and today, he didn't think twice before calling me a bastard. How quickly things have changed!

Mohanaswamy slowly rose from the bed, walked towards Karthik's room and started knocking on the door. There was no reply. 'I am sorry, Karthi,' he pleaded. Karthik wasn't moved. 'Please, my dear, I will never touch you again. I am sorry. It was my fault. Please don't be angry with me,' he implored. Still there was no reply from the other side. 'Henceforth, I will listen to whatever you say. Forgive me. Please allow me to sleep next to you. I promise I will not touch you,' Mohanaswamy begged. But Karthik did not open the door. Mohanaswamy even tried calling him on his mobile, but Karthik disconnected the call. When he redialled, the phone was switched off.

Clueless, Mohanaswamy went to the puja room. He sat in silence, staring at Krishna's idol. Then he took the idol in his hand and kissed it passionately on the lips. On the flute, on the chest and navel, waist and thighs … He showered kisses all over Krishna. 'Please change Karthi's mind, Krishna, I beg you. His rage will burn me to cinders. Without him, what's left for me in this world? Parting from him will be the death of me. Krishna, please understand the agony of your gopabala, this poor cowherd boy. Such silence and anger is unworthy of you. Forgive my sins and help me Krishna…' Mohanaswamy requested earnestly. Krishna stood playing his flute, with the same beguiling smile on his face. 'You are a cheat, Krishna … you are silent again. Well … I forgive you for this today, but not always … I'm warning you…' he threatened Krishna, delirious in his pain.

He returned to his room, closed the door and bolted it from inside. 'Karthi, I'll teach you a lesson. I'll make you starve today. I have feelings too,' he muttered. He made up his mind and sank into his bed. But the very next moment, his resolve weakened. Karthi may come anytime and knock on the door. What if I'm fast asleep then? What if my beloved Karthi is forced to go back to his room in frustration? Mohanaswamy panicked at the possibility. He jumped up, unbolted the door and kept it wide open. 'Karthi, to you, my heart's door will never close. None of your flaws will make me angry. In fact, I have no right, or the guts, to be angry with you. Come Karthi, come back to the room. You are always welcome. I will be waiting for you,' he said under his breath and staggered into the bed. But sleep eluded him again. He kept running to the loo and drinking water the whole night. However, given his fetish for cleanliness, every time he drank water, he washed the glass clean with soap, wiped it and kept it back on the shelf.

Finally, tired of waiting, Mohanaswamy curled up on the bare floor in front of Karthik's room. He lay wakeful in that position for the rest of the night, wallowing in self-pity. Finally, at the crack of dawn, he caught some sleep, a sickly sleep fraught with bad dreams.

When Karthik woke up, it was 7 a.m. He stretched his arms only to realize Mohanaswamy was not there next to him. He switched on his mobile phone. Six messages flowed in – five from Mohanaswamy which he deleted without even reading and the sixth from Rashmi, saying, 'Good morning, sweetheart'. 'How can my morning be good without you?' he texted her back and came out of the room, yawning and stretching.

When he saw Mohanaswamy sleeping on the cold floor, a wave of tenderness filled him and he felt sorry. 'I shouldn't have behaved so badly last night,' he muttered. Sitting next to him, he caressed Mohanaswamy's hair, bent over and kissed him lightly on his cheek.

Mohanaswamy slowly opened his eyes and asked, 'What's the time, Karthi?'

'There is still a lot of time. You better sleep. Today I will go and get milk and make coffee for you,' Karthik said, caressing his cheeks.

'No, no, you don't know how to boil milk, you will spill it over,' Mohanaswamy said and tried to get up.

'Shush! Idiot, sleep quietly. I will wake you up after the coffee is ready,' Karthik commanded, pushing him back to the floor.

Mohanaswamy smiled meekly, even as his eyes shone with happiness.

'Now don't smile, just sleep,' Karthik chided him.

Mohanaswamy took Karthik's hand and placed it on his chest, still smiling. Karthik slowly withdrew his hand, patted his cheek and walked towards the door to go out.

'Do you still love me?' Mohanaswamy asked, catching a glimpse of Karthik's tall masculine frame at the door.

'Shhhh!' Karthik put his finger to his mouth and said authoritatively, 'No talking. Just sleep until I'm back.' He winked mischievously at Mohanaswamy and stepped out of the house, shutting the door behind.

Mohanasawmy's day was made. Lying still on the floor, he thanked Krishna in his heart.

As Karthik ran down the stairs, his mobile beeped. Rashmi had texted back: 'In that case, come flying to me, my dear. We can be together for the entire day.' Karthik was thrilled. By the time he reached the milk booth, he had decided, 'After making coffee, I will take the first flight to Mumbai.'

~

Mohanaswamy gave the engagement ceremony a miss on the pretext of office work. Karthik too didn't insist that he attend. But Shobha aunty and her husband were quite upset. 'You are his best friend, how could you not come?' they asked. Many of Karthik's friends, who went to Mumbai to attend the function, had called him up to know why he wasn't there. Mohanaswamy grew tired of their nagging. He decided to attend the wedding ceremony just to avoid such unsavoury questions.

Meanwhile, Karthik stopped coming home. After office hours, he would go to Shobha aunty's house and stay over. When he met Mohanaswamy, he would say he was busy with the preparations for the wedding. Mohanaswamy was vexed as he received no responses to his repeated messages. Sometimes he would text Karthik, 'Are you doing okay? I don't want anything else. Just message me and let me know that you are doing fine. That's enough for me.' To this, if he was lucky, he would get a reply: 'I am doing fine. But busy'. This would make Mohanaswamy feel happy and light-hearted for a day. Perhaps Karthi is really busy. Getting married is not a joke. So much preparation goes into it. I know he is not the kind to ignore me, Mohanaswamy would console himself.

Sometimes he would prepare Karthik's favourite dishes. 'Today I have made bitter gourd curry. I know you love it. Please come home for dinner,' he would text Karthik. As usual there would be no reply. Still, Mohanaswamy would wait up for him. Finally, he would go to bed without eating.

One time Shobha aunty's house was full of guests and there was no place for Karthik to sleep. So, much to Mohanaswamy's delight, Karthik came home. A thrilled Mohanaswamy hovered around him with a spring in his step, talking about this and that, enthusiastically recounting the incidents that had taken place in Karthik's absence. But a stifling silence descended on the house when they switched off the lights and went to bed. Should I touch him or not? Mohanaswamy pondered. Bitter memories made him jittery.

Karthik was sleeping on his stomach, baring his back. The sight of his burly buttocks made Mohanaswamy's knees go weak. Flames of desire shot through him. His resolve fizzled out and lust got the better of his fears. He slowly placed his hand on Karthik's head. Then he ran his fingers over his bare back. There was no response.

'*Maunam sammati lakshanam*' – silence indicates agreement, he assumed. He slid his hands further down to his lower spine and began caressing gently.

And that was it! Karthik was incandescent with rage. He rose at once, grabbed Mohanaswamy's forearm and twisted it violently. Mohanaswamy shrieked out in pain. Annoyed further by his screams, Karthik twisted his smarting hand again. 'Stop it, Karthi, please stop it. Leave my hand, my bones will break,' Mohanaswamy pleaded pathetically. He couldn't do anything else apart from begging for mercy. He couldn't think of hitting him back, not even in his wildest dreams. 'Bolimagane, if you touch me again, I will chop your hands off!' Karthik shouted vehemently, stormed out of the house and went away on his bike.

Mohanaswamy was absolutely flabbergasted. Wincing with pain, he vowed not to touch Karthik again. 'Krishna, with you as my witness, I take an oath. I will never ever touch that rogue in my life. I will not even talk to him. Forget talking, I will not even think about him.'

His right hand hurt like hell the next day. He took leave from office and sat at home – alone, applying oil on his hand and sobbing. He thought of going to a doctor, but later decided against it because if the doctor asked how it happened, he would be in a fix. A simple 'sorry' message from Karthik would have soothed his wounds, but no such miracle took place. Suddenly, he was reminded of Shobha aunty. Perhaps she would understand his agony. 'I want to speak to you,' he messaged her. 'Sure. But not today. I am busy. Will speak tomorrow,' she replied. By evening, he thought it was ridiculous to tell her all that transpired between him and Karthik. He would only be making a fool of himself. He could share his pain with only one person – Lord Krishna.

'When shall we speak?' Shobha aunty sent a message with a smiley the next day. He didn't reply. She sent another text. Her inquisitiveness irked Mohanaswamy. 'Sorry, Aunty, it's nothing so important. Will tell you when we meet next,' he texted her and heaved a sigh of relief. 'As you wish. It was you who wanted to talk after all,' she sent a sarcastic message with an angry emoji.

For the next three days, Mohanaswamy didn't call or text Karthik. He decided he was never going to talk to him again. But the fourth day was 25 August. It was Karthik's birthday. All these years, they had celebrated his birthday together. Every year Karthik would book a room in a grand hotel to spend the night in a special way. Mohanaswamy would buy valuable gifts for him. So, how could he ignore Karthik on this occasion? Mohanaswamy found his mind wavering. He decided to buy a gift for him. I will go meet Karthi, hand over the gift and come back immediately. Then I will not think about him from tomorrow. I will not even talk to him. If he talks to me, that's different. Just because he twisted my hand in a fit of rage, I cannot sever my relations with him. If I blow this trivial issue out of proportion, even Krishna will not appreciate it. After all, my Karthi is not all that bad, he told himself.

He went to several malls in the city and finally chose an expensive shirt, a pair of branded trousers, a tie and innerwear and got them gift-wrapped. He then waited outside Karthik's office with the present in his hand. Mohanaswamy saw Karthik's Bajaj Pulsar parked outside. He mentally prepared himself to walk away after handing over the gift and never interfere in his life thereafter.

Karthik came out at 6 p.m., but he was not alone. There was a woman with him. He had his arms around her shoulder. It was none other than his fiancée, Rashmi. The moment Mohanaswamy realized it, his legs began quivering. They walked over to the bike together. Karthik combed his hair looking into the bike mirror. Rashmi patted his head affectionately. He then put on his helmet and she helped him fasten its belt. He said something at which she gave a light pat on his back. Karthik pretended as if he was hurt. Rashmi's smile was bright like lightning-flashes. Karthik looked at her in adoration. When he started the bike, she sat astride, holding him tightly from the behind with one hand and placing another hand on his thigh. Karthik leaned back and she rested her face on his shoulder. As Mohanaswamy looked on, they whizzed past the traffic ahead.

Mohanaswamy stood still. He felt dead on his feet and had no energy to go home. The gift pack lay limp in his hands. Overcome by an utter sense of defeat, he sat on the kerbstone for a long time, grieving. Finally, he gathered himself and got up to go. On his way home, he saw a beggar by the roadside. He walked up to him, dropped the gift pack into his hands and walked off quickly.

~

There was a big crowd of people at the wedding hall. Laughter and chatter filled the air as young and beautiful girls and boys walked around, flaunting their finery. Children were busy running around, squealing with joy. Disciplinarian elders were seen giving pep talks to vainglorious youths. Karthik's friends were teasing him. Karthik was dismissing and encouraging them in turn with his smiles and mock frowns.

Amidst all this garish happiness, Mohanaswamy feared he may break into tears any moment. Krishna, please dry these tears. Don't belittle me by making me cry in front of all these people, Mohanaswamy prayed earnestly.

'Why are you so quiet today?' some friends came and asked him.

'I am not feeling well,' he said, trying to avoid them.

'Why are you so dull? How will the wedding take place without you?' Shobha aunty also came and asked.

'The wedding will anyway take place aunty, whether I am there or not there,' he said, feeling empty within.

'Sometimes it is very difficult to understand you, Mohana,' Shobha aunty said and patted his head.

In the meantime, Karthik was introducing all his friends to Rashmi. Rashmi looked resplendent in a green silk sari. She was affable and graceful, speaking to everyone pleasantly, cracking jokes and lapping up all the attention. When his desire was the same as hers, how could the entire world support her this openly, putting her on a pedestal? Mohanaswamy could not help but wonder. But if I, even by the slip of my tongue, speak of my desires to the people gathered here, they will fling me to the ground and beat me to death, he thought.

Karthik came looking for Mohanaswamy. 'Did you have some snacks? Why are you sitting here alone?' he asked, showing concern. Then pointing to him, he asked Rashmi, 'Can you guess who this is?'

'Ummm…' Rashmi thought for a while and said, 'Mohanaswamy, right?'

'Yes,' said Mohanaswamy instantly.

She clapped her hands in glee. 'Karthik keeps talking about you so much that I sometimes envy you. He remembers you at least ten times a day. Mohana said this, Mohana said that … He goes on and on about you…' she said with a laugh.

'No, Mohana, she is lying. I never speak so much about you,' Karthik said curtly.

'See, already you have started lying to me. Men will be men after all!' she chided Karthik and turning to Mohanaswamy, she said, 'You please don't cultivate vices like him. Please be nice to women.' Mohanaswamy nodded his head. Just then Rashmi's friend called her. 'Excuse me,' Rashmi said and left.

Mohanaswamy shook Karthik's hand and said, 'Your selection is just too good, Karthik. You're a lucky man. Congrats.'

'Thanks, Mohana. Your saying it makes it very special for me,' Karthik said, placing his hand on Mohanaswamy's shoulder.

More guests came in. Rashmi's father was very rich. He had spent lavishly – after all, she was his only daughter. As the muhurtam, the auspicious hour, approached, the wedding hall resonated with Vedic hymns. Rashmi and Karthik religiously followed the priest's instructions. Then the band began playing the wedding music and Rashmi showered a handful of akshata – rice grains mixed with vermillion and turmeric – on Karthik's head. Karthik too put the akshata on her head.

After the ceremony, the crowd broke into different groups again. Shobha aunty picked a handful of rice grains from the floor and walked towards Karthik's friends who were standing in a group, chatting. 'It is said that on whoever's head this akshata is put, they will get married soon. They will get a good-looking bride. So tell me, who wants it first?' she asked jovially.

The boys jostled against one another to get the rice grains showered on their head. 'Put little more, Aunty,' some boys pleaded.

'If I put more, it's not like you will get two wives. Instead you will get one big fat wife!' Shobha aunty said, laughing at her own joke. Then her eyes fell on Mohanaswamy. 'Why are you standing aloof? Come, I will put rice grains on you,' she said, advancing towards him.

'No, Aunty, no, I don't want it,' he replied.

But the other boys pushed him towards her and said, 'Put akshata on him, Aunty. He wants to escape from marriage, that's not done.'

'No, Aunty, no, please, I beg you!' Mohanaswamy pleaded.

But Shobha aunty did not listen. She succeeded in showering the rice on his head.

'Hey!' All the boys screamed.

Mohanaswamy simply couldn't bear it. He ran from there, pushing his way through the crowd, as a searing pain shot through him. He felt as though the rice grains on his head were burning his hair, his skin, muscles and his heart. The imaginary stench of burning hair nauseated him. Feeling bilious, he ran out from the hall like a bat out of hell. There was a heap of stinking garbage by the roadside. He sat beside the heap and began dusting the rice grains off his head. The foul smell emanating from the garbage pile assailed his nostrils. He threw up everything he had eaten since morning. He puked and puked till water began streaming out of his nostrils. Then, sitting beside that stinking garbage heap, a stinking Mohanaswamy burst into sobs and moaned aloud. There was no one around to console him. Back at the wedding hall, everyone was busy congratulating the newlyweds.

It was Karthik and Rashmi's first night. Mohanaswamy lay curled up in bed, but couldn't sleep. He fantasized about Karthik copulating with Rashmi. He pictured them together, devouring each other's bodies with intermittent moans of pleasure and peals of laughter. Now Karthik has dedicated himself to her – all that he has is hers. Every particle of his body is now her property.

Why should I even think of all this? Why these voyeuristic instincts? No, I should not imagine all these things. It's his personal life. His passions, his desires belong to him alone!

And yet, he pictured Karthik being mesmerized by Rashmi's full breasts. He is holding them in his hands, fondling and caressing with insatiable desire. She has swept him off his feet. And now, how he is enjoying her, once tenderly, once roughly, and once…

No please, no. Let these images disappear from my mind! I want to sleep. I don't want him to come in my dreams. I don't want to touch him again, never in my life. I don't even want to think about him. Oh … look there, he is bathing her in kisses. He isn't repulsed upon touching any part of her body with his tongue. She is groaning, in ecstasy, in the frenzy of her orgasm. Now Karthik knows that she is the real, unalloyed gold. And all these days, what he considered gold was not genuine, it was fake. No, Karthik, no. Please don't do that. You are being unfair to me. I hate you. Please don't treat me like an insect!

With his face buried in her cunt, he will never keep any secrets from her. It's just a matter of a day or two. He will blurt out everything about me, my perverted and filthy ways. 'How silly!' he will laugh. She will be startled, disgusted. You silly creature, you have fallen in her eyes. Now, whenever she sees you, she will burst into laughter and Karthik will join in. She will tell everyone around and they will start laughing and scoffing at you. Vile jokes and laughter will follow in your wake wherever you go. You will diminish by the day and ultimately reduce into nothingness. They will only want to swat you, to get rid of the irritation.

No, no, please don't do that to me! I too want to live. Just give me a chance. I want to stay away from this madness. It's driving me crazy. It gives me nothing but pain. I will simply live, without sex. Eating, working and sleeping, that's it. Just leave me to myself. I will abstain from this infernal sex. I will win over it.

Oh, you fool, don't think of ways that are implausible. You say you will defy lust? Just feel the excitement that surges through you as you picture his naked body. Just one smile from him is enough to shake your determination. His manly gait is enough to enslave you. You only deserve to wait on him, to be at his beck and call, to get beaten up, to get kicked, to get scolded and to wallow in servitude. And then to wait eternally for that one fine day when he will come and touch you with love... You will keep waiting for that one moment. You will go on chasing him and end up frustrated. You will pine for him. You will grieve his absence. But no one will understand your grief. You will become the butt of their jokes. Your father, mother, sister, friends, colleagues, teachers, servants, society, office, court and the entire world – no one will accept or forgive you. You have fallen in their eyes. No one will pity you.

No, I don't want anything. I just want to sleep. Krishna, I have loved you with my heart, I have adored you. Don't give such a harsh punishment to your gopabala. Save me! I am drowning, save me, hold my arms and lift me up. And if you don't want me to live, kill me now, this very moment. No one will cry over my death, not even my family. I don't know why you brought this pain to me. What sin did I commit that warrants this pain?

Well, you are not going to help me, right? Let it be. I know you only enjoy playing your useless flute all the time. I shall find a solution to my pain. Look at this knife, this glistening knife. How it cuts deep into my thumb, a part of my body, which is your very own creation. Look here, Krishna, how the blood is oozing out. My blood is also red like Karthik's, let there be no doubts about it. You still don't believe me? Okay, I will anoint you with my blood. Until now, you have bathed only in milk, curd and honey. Today you will taste blood. But even that isn't new to you. You have bathed in blood before, every time you take birth on this earth, on the pretext of annihilating miscreants. You have lived as ten avatars and I know you are quite proud. Now I believe you are all eager to take your eleventh incarnation. If so, I will give you a curse. Accept it...

In your eleventh avatar, you will take birth like me. Yes, like me, a faint-hearted creature, a weakling. You have enjoyed sixteen thousand women before. Now, you will know how painful it is to be in a position where no one desires you. In this avatar, when you are too weak to even raise your hand on anyone, I will see how you annihilate wrong-doers. You will be a worm in the eyes of others. Just like me. And you will suffer your pain in silence. Just like me.

~

Finally, on the fourth day, Mohanaswamy managed to get some sleep. The main reason for this was a twenty-eight-year-old youth called Raghuraman, whom Mohanaswamy had got acquainted with through the internet. Hailing from Coimbatore, he now lived in Bengaluru and taught in an international school. He had a house in Basavanagudi where he lived alone.

During the chat, he had asked for Mohanaswamy's photo. After hesitating for a while, Mohanaswamy shared his photo with him. 'You look smart, buddy,' came the reply. Raghuraman had uploaded about eighteen pictures of himself on the blog. He looked nice in a couple of them.

They decided to meet at 7 p.m. on Friday at the Coffee Day in Sheshadripuram. Mohanaswamy sent him the route map, meticulously marking all landmarks and crosses en route – a cinema hall, a super market and the one-way roads. 'You are so organized, I like it!' came the reply. Raghuraman shared his mobile number and asked for Mohanaswamy's. But Mohanaswamy said he would give it only after meeting him.

Mohanaswamy was half an hour early to Coffee Day. He had purchased a new sim card for his mobile and had memorized the number. He had inserted two condoms in his pocket, should the necessity arise. I must accept Raghuraman, no matter how he turns out to be. If minds don't meet, it is impossible for bodies to come together. But I should be on my guard. I must not allow oral sex. After meeting once or twice, when trust is built, I must take him to a hospital to get an HIV test done. But I am not taking him home at any cost. And neither will I go to his room, even if he insists. It will be safer to book a room in a hotel.

Raghuraman came in at seven, dressed in a pink suit. Looking around, he spotted Mohanaswamy and walked towards his table, smiling. He sat in the chair opposite him and waving his hands, said, 'Horrible traffic you know!' Mohanaswamy was utterly disappointed at the way Raghuraman came in, walking and swaying. His dressing sense and gestures were quite effeminate.

No, I will not get into this relationship, Mohanaswamy decided.

'What have you done to your hand?' asked Raghuraman tenderly.

'Just a small injury. I cut my hand while chopping vegetables.'

'Oh my god! You should be careful,' he said, placing

his palms on his cheeks. He took Mohanaswamy's hand, caressed the bandage and asked, 'Is it paining a lot?' Mohanaswamy shook his head.

They ordered cappuccinos. 'Shall I ask for samosas?' asked Mohanaswamy.

'No, baba, I am dieting,' said Raghuraman coquettishly.

Some incongruous discussions followed. Raghuraman said something about Tamil cinema, but Mohanaswamy did not know anything or anyone except Rajinikanth. Mohanaswamy spoke about cookery, but Raghuraman pointed to the fat content in each of the recipes. He loved Carnatic music, but Mohanaswamy had no taste for music other than Hindi film songs. Luckily, both had no interest in cricket. They grew weary and frustrated after spending half an hour at the cafe. Mohanaswamy wanted to pay the bill, but Raghuraman stopped him. He walked straight to the counter and paid the bill. While tipping the waiter, he said, 'Wonderful interiors.'

Before they parted, Raghuraman asked him, 'Can I have your mobile number?'

Mohanaswamy reluctantly gave him a missed call. Anyway, it is a new sim, so I can throw it away tomorrow if need be, he thought.

'How did you come here? I can drop you home if you want,' Raghuraman offered.

'No, thanks. My house is quite far. I will take the bus,' replied Mohanaswamy, desperate to wriggle out.

'We had a wonderful time together. It was nice meeting you,' Raghuraman took his hand, slowly lifted it to his mouth and planted a kiss on it.

Every hair on Mohanaswamy's body stood on its end in disgust. He looked over his shoulders to see whether people were watching. He sighed in relief as no one seemed to be bothered about them.

Mohanaswamy headed back home, disappointed. The unused condoms in his pocket seemed to be mocking him. After all this waiting and anxiety, I ended up meeting such a sissy. How can I share my body with a person like this? If such a person touches me, my body responds in disgust, forget being aroused. No I can't have any relationship with him. He can never measure up to my Karthi. No comparison between my Karthi – who makes a woman's heart curl up like a shy bud with his glance – and this idiot, who walks so coyly! No, not possible. Tomorrow I will message him and say I am not interested.

Just then, his mobile beeped. A message had landed. It must be from Raghuraman. 'Don't feel sad, Mohanaswamy, but I am in search of a man who is as strong as a bull. But the way you sat, the way you spoke –

I found too many feminine qualities in you. How can I share my body with you? If my decision has hurt you, please forgive me. You are a very nice person. I'm sure you will find a good man for yourself,' Raghuraman had texted.

Mohanaswamy was stumped. For a moment, he didn't know what to do. Then, he pulled himself together and shot back a reply: 'I wish good luck to you too. You are a nice person too. I love you.'

'I love you too,' pat came the reply.

Mohanaswamy took out the sim from his mobile, broke it into two pieces and threw them out of the window of the bus. He laughed at the irony of the situation. I'll surely get some sleep tonight, he thought. Then he gently rested his head against the windowpane and closed his eyes.

BICYCLE RIDING

If I learn to ride a bicycle, I will turn from gay to straight.

When this thought flashed across twenty-one-year-old Mohanaswamy's mind, a dark night had descended on the coastal state of Goa. Huge waves were crashing down on the seashore. As Mohanaswamy tossed and turned on the bed in a hotel room in that unfamiliar city, his friends, tired of cycling and braving the hot sun the whole day, were slipping into deep sleep one by one. Elsewhere in the city, owners of wine and mutton shops were downing their shutters.

It was just about two years ago that Mohanaswamy had come across the word 'gay'. He now identified himself with that word, though he wasn't sure whether it really described him. For him, 'straight' meant every other creature on earth except him and the people of his ilk. English dailies and magazines like *Debonair* often used the word 'gay'. But he didn't know what gays were called in the vernacular. So far he had earned several monikers in the local slang – each one filling him with pain, disgust, humiliation and incredulity. But there was no equivalent word for 'gay' in Kannada. You wouldn't even find it in dictionaries and newspapers.

The first moniker Mohanaswamy got was 'GanSu', a short form for 'Gandu Sule', which, in Kannada, referred to a male prostitute. Shockingly, it was his sister, Janaki, who gave him the horrendous nickname. He was a schoolboy then, studying in the seventh standard. Even now, Mohanaswamy wondered whether his sister really knew the meaning of the word or she uttered it inadvertently. It was a hot summer day. A lunch had been organized for the Brahmin families of his village at the Raghavendraswamy temple. Mohanaswamy's parents had left for the temple at ten in the morning, asking the children to join them at lunchtime. Janaki's friends had come home to play. Mohanaswamy loved to play house with those girls. He found it more interesting than playing gilli-danda, top and marbles with boys. Though the girls forced him to go and play with boys, he wouldn't listen. The boys always bullied him. That day too, he hung around with the girls at their doll's wedding. They drew rangoli designs on the floor, wrapped towels around their waists as saris and tapped their feet as they sang songs. They did not notice how much time had gone by in fun and frolic until Mohanaswamy alerted that it was past twelve o' clock and time to leave for the temple.

If you walk barefoot on a hot summer day on the streets in Ballari district, your soles will develop boils by the time you take ten steps. The children had no other option but to walk barefoot as their lower middle class parents never bought them slippers, fearing that they might lose them while playing outdoors. So Mohanaswamy and the girls started walking barefoot. They chatted along the way, ran when they couldn't bear the heat and stopped by under the shade of tamarind trees intermittently. As they walked, they came across a small canal, which had to be crossed to reach the temple located on the other side. A little further, a stone slab was put across the drain to facilitate the crossing of it. But to reach the slab, people had to walk a couple of yards ahead. Already exhausted, the children were in no mood to walk any further. They stopped by the canal and some of the girls hesitated to step on the slab in case they spoilt their ghagra-cholis. The canal carried human excreta and filth of the entire town.

Leaving his sister and her friends behind, Mohanaswamy, bubbling with enthusiasm, ran towards the canal in great speed and jumped over it successfully, like Hanuman vaulting the ocean. The girls watched him aghast. 'Come on! Jump over, just like me. Can you do it?' Mohanaswamy screamed, standing at the other end of the drain. A couple of girls in the group tried to imitate him in vain. Others hesitated even to try. 'Losers! Losers!' Mohanaswamy screamed, giving them the thumbs down. 'I am the winner, I am the winner,' he yelped in joy. The girls were offended. Seeing him jumping around in joy, and in a bid to defend her team, Janaki yelled at him, 'Stop it! Why are you dancing like this? Are you a prostitute? Yes, you are Gandu Sule, a male prostitute!'

Shocked, Mohanaswamy held his breath and steadied himself. His sister's harsh words, followed by the laughter of the girls, pierced his ears. Encouraged further by her friends' response, Janaki repeated the word even louder. 'Gandu Sule!'

The incident left an indelible mark on Mohanaswamy's psyche. But his new moniker intrigued elders as well as youngsters in the town. They shortened it to 'GanSu'. From guilt and shame, Mohanaswamy lost confidence in whatever he did. He wondered whether he would ever be able to vault over the canal again. One day, just to reassure himself, he walked alone towards the canal and attempted to jump over it. But he fell into the filthy water. He went home and scrubbed his body with soap over and over again and poured buckets of water over himself. But the stench lingered on for over a week. Thereafter, whenever he recollected the incident, he felt the dirty water still dripping from all over his body and the stink assaulting his nostrils.

~

Mohanaswamy abhorred people calling him 'GanSu', but he lacked the courage to stop them. Despite his pleas, people continued to tease him. Helpless, he decided to ignore them. But then something worse happened. That day he was back home after writing his mathematics exam in school. Though Mohanaswamy was good in other subjects, he found maths a tough nut to crack. He hated solving those arithmetic sums, algebraic equations and geometry theorems. Knowing his weakness in maths, his mother, who had studied till tenth standard, sat with him in the evenings and helped him with the subject. That day, after he came back from the exam, his mother was waiting for him in the frontyard, doing her chores. Mohanaswamy knew it was going to be a bad day for him as he had not done well in the exam. He sat quietly, lowering his head as his mother began scrutinizing him.

She solved all the questions one by one and tallied his answers against the correct answers. When she added up the marks, it came to only 48 out of 100. Incandescent with rage, she thrashed him black and blue with a steel plate lying on the floor.

'I'm sorry, Amma, please forgive me,' Mohanaswamy cried in despair.

But his mother did not relent. 'I toiled so hard to teach you, but still you did so badly in the exam,' she screamed, tears flowing down her cheeks. She beat him till the bangles on her forearms broke. Then, exhausted, she flung the steel plate away and sat weeping. Mohanaswamy too wept loudly.

After some time, his mother screamed at the top of her voice, 'You bloody fool, you know how to dance like a prostitute, but you don't know how to solve these sums? You bloody GanSu!'

A shocked Mohanaswamy looked at her in total disbelief. Her words pierced through him like a sword. He had not expected it from his mother. In fact, it was she who came to his rescue whenever his sister called him GanSu. 'He is a boy. Don't offend him like that. If I hear you using that dirty word again, I won't spare you,' she would warn. But that day Mohanaswamy's whole world came crashing down. He felt as if God himself had deceived him.

Realizing how harsh she had been, his mother felt sorry for him. 'Stop crying now,' she gruffly ordered him, trying to put up a straight face. But he did not stop. She tried to hug him. He brushed her hands off his shoulders. 'Please stop crying, darling,' she said in a soft voice, wiping his tears. Her soothing words intensified his grief and he wept louder. 'Please don't cry, my boy, I am so sorry, please forgive me. I promise I will never call you that again. I never intended to … the word slipped off my tongue in a fit of rage,' she cried. They wept in each other's arms. After a while, his mother said, 'Come, let's have lunch. I have prepared your favourite dry methi-daal curry.' Mohanaswamy followed her. After all, he couldn't resist the temptation of the methi-daal curry, the aroma of fenugreek leaves, tur daal and grated coconut that was already filling the room. His mother made him sit in front of her, and instead of serving food in a plate as usual, she lovingly put the morsels in his hand, watching him swallow them one by one.

'You are so good at other subjects, but why are you scared of mathematics?' she asked him gently, putting a morsel in his hand. Gulping it down, Mohanaswamy looked her in the eye and asked, 'Tell me, Amma, what's the meaning of Gandu Sule? Why do people call me so?'

'Forget it, my son. It is nonsense. Why should anybody call you so? You are not a prostitute. You will grow up into a strong, handsome man, who can keep a hundred prostitutes,' she said, trying to boost his mood.

'But why do people target only me?' Mohanaswamy asked naively. 'I haven't heard them name-calling any of the other boys.'

His mother did not know what to say. After a while she replied, 'You must also behave like boys. Then nobody will dare call you so.'

'But how to behave like boys, Amma?'

'The way you speak, the way your voice sounds, the movement of your eyes, your body language, the games you play ... everything should be like that of boys.'

'But who taught the other boys all that? Nobody taught me.'

'Why would anybody teach such things? God teaches them everything before sending them to earth.'

'Then, why didn't God teach me? What was my fault?'

Silence descended on them for a while. Tears rolled down his mother's cheeks as she dropped the morsel in the bowl.

'Why are you crying, Amma?' Mohanaswamy asked in concern.

'It was not your fault, my boy. We are the culprits – myself and your father. It was our fault,' she said, sobbing.

'What was your fault?'

'They say children born to older parents end up in a

garbage bin. We didn't realize it then,' she said, staring at the ceiling.

Mohanaswamy did not understand what she was trying to say.

'Tell me, what is your father's age now?' she asked him.

'I don't know,' said Mohanaswamy.

'On the second day after this Ugadi, your father will be seventy. Now tell me, how old are you?' she asked him.

'I am thirteen,' said Mohanaswamy.

'That means, when you were born, your father was fifty-seven. I was nearing forty. It was his second marriage. I had remained unmarried for long. So I agreed to marry him though he was much older than me. But age never comes in the way of men's desires. I told him not to go for a second child at that age. But he did not listen. So you were born. What to do? It is all my karma,' she sighed.

Mohanaswamy was too young to comprehend what his mother was trying to say. All that he understood was that he was made to suffer because of his father's desire. But he loved his father. He was such a gentleman, always kind. And he never abused or beat Mohanaswamy. So it was hard for him to think ill of him.

Yet another ugly scene unfolded at home one night which changed the way Mohanaswamy perceived life. His father was out of town for some work. The three of them had just finished dinner. Janaki usually cleared the plates from the floor and mopped it. She hated doing it but had no choice. That night, she was looking for some excuse to skip the work. She had bought some mehendi to apply on her hands and so, after dinner, she quietly went and sat in a corner mixing the mehendi. The plates were lying on the floor for quite some time.

'Why have you not put away these dirty plates yet? Can't you see they are drying up? If you leave them to dry, evil may befall us,' her mother shouted from the kitchen.

Janaki, who was busy mixing mehendi, told Mohanaswamy, 'Oye, GanSu, please, you do this task for me today.'

To this Mohanaswamy firmly said, 'I won't do it. It's not a man's job.'

'Oh! So you call yourself a man? You are not a man, you are a GanSu, just a GanSu, GanSu…' she said in a singsong.

His mother came out rushing with a steel ladle in her hand. 'Bosudi … How many times have I told you not to call him so? Why are you abusing the son of the house?' she lashed out and beat the girl vehemently with the ladle. Janaki was taken aback by this sudden attack. Mohanaswamy too found their mother's rage out of proportion. He stood watching the scene in disbelief.

'Don't beat me, Amma, I will never repeat it again...' the girl pleaded, wincing in pain.

Exhausted, the mother finally threw the ladle in a corner and sat on the floor leaning against a pillar. 'It's just my fate...' she murmured, weeping loudly.

With bruises and welts on her body, Janaki wept furiously. Grief and shame rose up inside Mohanaswamy as he cursed himself for being the root cause of all the tension at home. It was his feminine mannerism that had destroyed the peace at home. He slowly rose from his place and went to clear the plates. His mother and sister watched him as he cleaned the floor, gathering the rice spilled over the sides of the plates. They were too spent to say anything.

~

Mohanaswamy decided to change himself. Since his feminine traits were the underlying cause of all the trouble, he made up his mind to be rough and tough, but he behaved like a robot instead, controlling the movement of his hands, legs and eyes. He also had to do something about his shrill voice. Since he couldn't change it, he thought the best solution was to talk less. He stopped asking questions in class. He stopped chitchatting with his classmates. He tried to speak in a low, harsh voice. 'Speak up, Mohana,' people would tell him. But he would speak with the same hoarseness. He had earned the nickname 'GanSu' because he played with his sister and her friends, so he stopped playing with them. If he went to play with the boys, they bullied him. So he decided to be all by himself. He read books. Sometimes he felt too tempted to join his sister and her friends, but he restrained himself.

There was yet another change in him. He had realized if he had scored well in mathematics, his loving mother would not have called him 'GanSu'. So he started paying more attention in the math class. With no friends to play and spend time with, he solved math problems when he got bored. All these efforts paid off. In his eighth standard, he topped the district and got full marks in maths, making his teachers and parents proud. He sort of became a role model in the town and people began advising their children to emulate Mohanaswamy, be as hardworking and sincere as him. He was felicitated in a couple of programmes in the district. All this pampering and recognition opened up a whole new world before Mohanaswamy. He had realized that if he had to escape from his shameful nickname 'GanSu', he must study hard and be recognized as an intelligent student. He stuck to his lessons firmly, like a blood-sucking leech.

His mother, though happy with her son's academic achievements, began missing the old Mohanaswamy whom she had to chide during the evening math lessons. There was nothing left for her to teach him. She felt as if her son was drifting away from her.

She remembered how she fed Mohanaswamy as a toddler, carrying him on her hip, showing him the moon above in the sky, putting the morsels in his mouth. Till he came to second standard, Mohanaswamy would only eat his meals outdoors, while watching the moon. He found it very difficult to have food on amavasya when there was no moon in the sky or when it hid behind clouds. But when Mohanaswamy reached second standard, he started eating on his own. If his mother offered to carry him outside and feed him like she used to do before, he would feel shy and refuse to go.

~

'If the wife comes on top during intercourse, boys with feminine qualities will be born.'

'Is it?' asked Mohanaswamy in a shivering voice as he walked one evening on the beach in front of his college, chatting with his classmate Sumit Goel, a handsome boy from Uttar Pradesh.

Just then a man with feminine mannerisms had walked past them. 'He is gay,' Sumit said, pointing to him. 'Do you know what the gays do?' he asked Mohanaswamy, winking.

Mohanaswamy nodded his head. He had heard the 'gay' word only recently. He had seen boys from big cities and those who studied in convents using the word and laughing about it. Eager to educate Mohanaswamy, Sumit whispered in his ears, 'They have sex with men.'

Mohanaswamy stiffened his body so as to hide his own girlish gait. He then feigned innocence and asked curiously, 'Tell me, why do they do like that?'

'They are sex maniacs. They are not satisfied having sex with women. So they sleep around with men too,' Sumit said, as if he knew all about sex.

'But are they born that way?' asked Mohanaswamy inquisitively.

Sumit said, it all depended on positions during sex. 'Such children are born when the woman comes on top. That's why I never allow girls to mount me. You must also keep this in mind: never allow girls to call the shots. Be careful,' Sumit advised him, proudly showing off his knowledge.

Why did my mother mount my father? Why did she commit such a blunder? Mohanaswamy pondered. The question drilled his brain like a woodpecker. He did not dare share his agony with Sumit or anyone else for the fear of being found out.

Mohanaswamy, who had hardly stepped out of Ballari district, did not know that north Indian boys looked so attractive. And now when he saw them in college, he was mesmerized by their fair complexion, their height, their dense hair and their flashy smiles which he found charming. He was stunned by the way they mingled freely with girls, drank in pubs and watched blue films. They were so bold, so different. South Indian boys looked somewhat dull and even juvenile compared to them.

Mohanaswamy had secured admission into that prestigious college in the coastal city because he had passed his second pre-university exams with flying colours. The college attracted a number of outstation students and Sumit Goel from Lucknow was one of them. He and Mohanaswamy were in the same course and they soon became friends. Sumit was not so keen on studies, his passion lay in cricket. He would practise day and night in the college grounds. He would skip exams and go to different cities to play tournaments. He cherished the dream of playing for the country. He found a good companion in Mohanaswamy, who patiently lent him an ear. Besides, Sumit found his association with Mohanaswamy quite useful. Mohanaswamy, the straight-A student would give him his neatly written notes. He would even write down lab sheets for Sumit. He would guess the probable questions before each exam and help Sumit prepare. He never expected anything in return.

Unlike the other boys in college, Mohanaswamy wasn't the drinking, outgoing type. He never looked at girls. He spoke less and was very shy. Sumit grew fond of this sober, studious, disciplined boy. Sometimes he would hug him affectionately, plant a kiss on his forehead and exclaim, 'If you were a girl, Mohana, I would have married you!' This would leave Mohanaswamy blushing.

Mohanaswamy was of course completely besotted with Sumit. He loved to be around him all the time. He went with him for evening strolls on the beach. If he bunked classes, Mohanaswamy would admonish him authoritatively. He accompanied him to the cricket grounds and cheered for him during the match and consoled him when he lost. Sumit was quite popular in college, especially with the girls. The grapevine was abuzz with rumours that he was going steady with some girl. Sumit would not refute these rumours. In fact, he often narrated his colourful encounters. Once, when Mohanaswamy refused to believe his stories, Sumit mischievously fished out two condoms from his pocket and showed them to Mohanaswamy saying, 'These are for tonight.'

Another time, during such a conversation, Sumit asked him, 'Have you ever fucked a girl?'

Mohanaswamy was taken aback by this sudden, direct question. He decided to pull a fast one. He said he was once in love with a girl in his town and was also physically involved with her.

'Oh! Not bad! On the outside you look so quiet and shy, but still waters run deep!' Sumit exclaimed with a naughty smile.

Of late, in a bid to conceal his true identity, Mohanaswamy had started joining the boys in their vulgar talk, raving about some girls' looks and passing lewd comments about movie stars. But behind this mask of machismo, his heart pined for the well-built boys in his class. But if he proclaimed it, he knew he would be ostracized. He was also tired of living this pretentious life, weaving lies with more lies. In the Mahabharata, Lord Krishna beheaded Shishupala with the Sudarshan Chakra for transgressing over a hundred times. I tell at least ten lies a day. What would be my fate? The nagging question often gave him sleepless nights.

Mohanaswamy would go for evening strolls on the beach with Sumit at every opportunity. With the Arabian Sea roaring, Mohanaswamy's heart would miss a beat if Sumit put his hand on his shoulder. Their conversations revolved around girls and sex. He often pestered Sumit to take him to the beach and on days when Sumit had no girlfriends to keep him company, he would yield to his requests. Mohanaswamy would set out for the beach stroll after bathing with Mysore Sandal soap. Sumit would have just come back from playing cricket, sweating profusely. The odour of the sweat would make Mohanaswamy burn with desire. Sumit would keep two of his shirt buttons open and expose his broad chest to the cool breeze. As he stretched his arms and enjoyed the breeze, he looked like a Gandharva. Mohanaswamy would feel like putting his arm around Sumit's shoulder. But Sumit was about ten inches taller than him. Mohanaswamy knew that he should not crave for something that was beyond his reach.

This was the eighties and the students would somehow secure low-grade detective novels with erotic descriptions and magazines like *Surathi* and *Rathi Vignyana* with pictures of nude women. They would circulate the forbidden books, read them till they were soiled and torn. While this was the plight of Kannada-speaking boys, the condition of boys from English medium schools was no different. The only contrast was that the books and periodicals they read were more glossy and attractive with full-colour spreads.

Mohanaswamy too would read such magazines with his mouth wide open. He would read them from start to end, hoping to find something, anything on gays. But in vain. Even when he did find some piece of information here and there, it would be so horrifying that it would give rise to a sense of shame in him. Once, he found a query in a magazine where the reader had mentioned that he was attracted to men and sought remedy for 'this tendency'. The agony aunt had answered to his query thus: 'Such desire crops up in men's mind due to affliction of Naga Dosha. Naga, the serpent god, is the one who blesses men with progeny. It appears that one of your forefathers killed a snake long ago. So you have incurred the curse of the snake god. You will be redeemed of the curse if you perform Naga puja every day.'

Dreaded cobras, with their hoods wide open, began haunting Mohanaswamy in his dreams. He started going to the Shiva temple every day, and prayed fervently to the idols of snakes inside its premises. But even after six months of Naga puja, nothing changed inside him. He was the same Mohanaswamy, whose organ would stand erect at the sight of boys in the hostel who would come out from the bathrooms, their bodies still glistening with water.

The boys hardly ever discussed homosexuality. Mohanaswamy never raised such topics on his own because that would give rise to unnecessary doubts in his friends' minds. So when gay sex did come up in their conversations, he would pass a snide remark or two as defence mechanism. But whenever somebody said something at length about homosexuality, he would be all ears. There was a boy in his class from Bengaluru, who boasted of his knowledge about sex, which he claimed to have acquired by reading English books and magazines. Once he gave a weird explanation for gayness in men. He said, 'Men tend to have a sexual orientation to persons of the same sex because of some defective chromosomes. If nature identifies some men as weak, it selects not to continue their lineage. So they are made born weak and cannot have sex with women and produce children. So their lineage will end with them.'

Mohanaswamy found this explanation too hard to digest. I am a very good boy. I am a diligent student. I haven't done anything bad to anybody. What have I done that natural selection plans to finish my lineage? Even fraudsters and crooks beget children. Am I worse than them? The question baffled him for a long time.

One day there was a telegram for Sumit with a message that his father had passed away. Sumit borrowed money from his friends and rushed to Lucknow for two weeks for the funeral. When he was away, Mohanaswamy was very sad thinking about the ill-fate that had befallen his friend. He decided to take better care of the fatherless boy. I should console him once he comes back. If he needs money I should help him out without thinking twice, he thought. He waited for Sumit's arrival with anxiety.

One day when he was working in the hydraulic lab, a friend came and told him that Sumit was back. On hearing the news, Mohanaswamy could not concentrate on his work. He rushed back to the hostel on the pretext of a headache. He headed to Sumit's room and pushed the door. Sumit was eating some sweets and happily dancing to the tune of a song playing on the radio.

'Hi, buddy, come inside,' Sumit welcomed him. 'Have a laddoo, it's very tasty,' he said, giving him a sweet.

Mohanaswamy was dumbstruck. Was it a lie that his father passed away? he wondered. 'Tell me, why did you go to Lucknow?' Mohanaswamy asked.

'Don't you know my father died?' Sumit replied, biting into one more laddoo.

'Aren't you sad that your father is no more?' Mohanaswamy asked in concern, unable to eat the laddoo.

Sumit laughed. 'No, not at all. In fact, it was good riddance. He harassed my mother a lot. He was bedridden since the past two years and my mother was exhausted taking care of him. Now she will live happily,' he said without any hesitation.

'How old was he?' Mohanaswamy asked hesitatingly.

'He was eighty-five. My mother was his third wife. The first two had died unable to bear his torture. My mother was lucky, she somehow survived. But he had made her life miserable. It seems when I was born, my father was already sixty-five. What to say of that bloody old man's lust even at that age! It seems even when he was bedridden, if any girls passed in front of him, he would set his lecherous eyes on them,' Sumit said venomously.

By then the radio started playing one of his favourite songs. 'Come on, let's dance!' Sumit said, wrapping his arm around Mohanaswamy's waist.

The incident demystified Mohanaswamy's notion that the perceived defects in his own personality were the result of his father's lust in old age. Sumit is also born of old parents. But he is so manly and strong, girls fall for him, wherever he goes, Mohanaswamy thought. As he realized that his mother's theory did not hold water, he felt relieved that his father was not the cause of his problem. He joyously danced with Sumit, grabbing him by his waist.

~

Mohanaswamy's friendship with Sumit ended on a bitter note when they were in the seventh semester. The separation was very painful and it took a long time for him to come out of his grief.

Mohanaswamy always knew his limits. Though Sumit's body attracted him like a magnet, he suppressed his feelings and mingled with him just like a friend. He had decided not to open up unless Sumit came forward and expressed his feelings. However, one day things went out of hand. That night Sumit had come back to the hostel, drunk. They had an exam on mechanical vibrations the next morning. Mohanaswamy tried to persuade him to skip the test. 'Today you are drunk. Just skip this exam. Anyway you will be given another chance to clear the backlog,' he said. But Sumit would not listen. 'No way,' he said. 'The university cricket match will coincide at the time of the third exams. I have to leave for Bengaluru. Tomorrow I must write the exam. Please help me study for it,' he pleaded, hugging Mohanaswamy and kissing him on the forehead. That was enough to persuade Mohanaswamy. He agreed to help Sumit.

That night Mohanaswamy's roommate was also seriously studying for the exam. They decided to sit in Sumit's room as his roommate had gone out of station and there was no one to disturb them. Mohanaswamy patiently explained the answers to him till two in the morning. Mohanaswamy was surprised that even in his inebriated condition, Sumit quickly grasped all that Mohanaswamy explained. He even asked questions that stumped Mohanaswamy. When the clock struck two, Mohanaswamy said, 'Sumit, enough of studying. Just write whatever you remember. What if you feel sleepy during the exam?' Yawning and stretching, he got up to go to his room.

Sumit was probably overwhelmed with gratitude towards Mohanaswamy and so he said, 'Tonight you sleep here, Mohana. You are also tired. Anyway my roommate is not there.'

'No, Sumit, I feel comfortable in my room,' Mohanaswamy said, walking towards the door. He did not want to embarrass himself.

'Please don't hurt me, my friend,' Sumit begged, holding his hands. This melted Mohanaswamy's heart and kindled a desire in him. He agreed to stay back.

In Sumit's room, two beds were kept adjacent to each other under the fan so that both Sumit and his roommate could sleep directly under the fan. Sumit was still under the influence of alcohol. He felt affectionate towards his friend Mohanaswamy for helping him out for the test. Switching off the lights, he pulled Mohanaswamy to his bed. Drawing him towards his chest and caressing his head affectionately, Sumit murmured, 'You are so good, my friend. You are so kind to me. You have been helping me all along. What can I give you in return?' Saying so, he passed out, his right leg still wrapped across Mohanaswamy's waist.

Mohanaswamy thought Sumit was indirectly inviting him. The body that he craved for since the past three years was right there next to him in that dark room. His hot breath mixed with the smell of alcohol and sweat ignited his desires. Mohanaswamy felt Sumit's private organ pressing against his waist. It was a dark amavasya night. The rhythm of sea waves drowned the sound of the fan.

Mohanaswamy could not resist the temptation any more. His body was quivering with desire, small waves were rising in the sea. He slowly turned towards Sumit and kissed his cheeks. A small wave crushed on the sea shore. He kissed Sumit's eyelids. Now a bigger wave pounded the sea shore. His hands ran over Sumit's body. A small ship was floating in the heart of the sea, riding the rising and falling waves. Groping in the dark, his hands strayed to Sumit's pyjamas and undid the stings. Deep down under the ocean, a shark caught a big fish and gulped it down.

Sumit woke up at this touch. For some time, he was disoriented. There was darkness everywhere. Did I drink excessively last night? It looks like I don't have any clothes on my body. Who is sleeping and moaning next to me? he thought. Slowly he realized that it was Mohanaswamy. 'What is he doing … thoo … he is a chakka…' he muttered, feeling disgusted.

Sumit felt like he had fallen into a filthy sewage canal. He had not expected this turn in their friendship. He used to hug and love Mohanaswamy the way he would his pet dog. He had a great deal of affection for Mohanaswamy, but now the bonhomie vanished into thin air and a sense of betrayal and disgust pervaded. Gently pushing Mohanaswamy aside, he sat up on the bed and put his vest back on. He pulled his bed away from under the fan and placed it closer to the wall. And even though it was very muggy in the room, he covered himself up with a sheet. Sleep eluded him. His mind wallowed in nausea. The experience was akin to mixing urine in holy water. After some time, he heard Mohanaswamy sobbing. For a moment, he felt sorry for him and thought of consoling him. But he decided he did not have anything to do with that coward who was neither a man nor a woman. He firmed up his mind. Mohanaswamy continued sobbing. Sumit pulled his sheet up further.

After a while, he heard Mohanaswamy getting up from the bed and folding his sheet. He decided to slap him across the face if he came near. But then he heard him walking towards the door and unlocking the bolt. Sumit felt miserable. He realized that Mohanaswamy was going back to his room and he called out, 'Mohana,' he said with a heart of stone. Mohanaswamy waited at the door. 'Mohana, I wish you all the best. Please don't talk to me ever in life. I don't like all this,' he begged. Without uttering a word, Mohanaswamy went away, closing the door behind him.

The ship floating in the middle of the sea was caught in massive waves. Even if people in the ship cried for help, Sumit, who was lying on the bed under the sheet, could never hear it. It was a cry in the wilderness. It was more helpless than the cry of the sea.

The next day, Mohanaswamy was absent. It was the first time in his life that he gave an exam a miss.

The wound inflicted by Sumit Goel took months to heal. Mohanaswamy had no one to share his woes with. He would go the beach alone and sit there, crying. Sometimes he would go to bed without having dinner. Somewhere in his mind, he still hoped that Sumit would have a change of heart and come back. But no such miracle took place. Whenever Sumit encountered him in the campus, he would not even look at him.

Sumit had long, thick hair. He would not go to saloon to cut it even if it grew till his neck. When he finished cricket practice in the evenings, sweat would be dripping from his hair strands. When Mohanaswamy came near him, he would shake his head like mad so the drops of sweat from his hair would fall on Mohanaswamy. Mohanaswamy would pretend to be angry, but secretly he used to like it. Now Mohanaswamy would go to the cricket ground in the evenings to relive the sweet memories. But Sumit would walk off without even looking at him.

When it was time for the next set of exams, Mohanaswamy thought Sumit would surely come to him for help. But nothing of the sort happened. In fact, Sumit passed with good marks.

Mohanaswamy pined for Sumit for a couple of months. He grew weary of life. Reeling under crippling feelings of loneliness and depression, he decided to end his life by drowning in the sea. He walked towards the seashore one night. The beach was deserted. He did not know how to swim. His plan was to walk into the sea and drown. He had thought of leaving a suicide note behind, holding Sumit Goel responsible for his death, but then decided against it. Mohanaswamy could not hate anybody. All he knew was love and friendship. In his mind, he wished all good things for Sumit and walked towards the roaring sea. It was a full moon night. As he stepped into the water, a sudden fear of death gripped him. Still, he kept walking adamantly till the water level reached his chest. It was then that he heard the shrieks of a woman. 'Who is it walking so deep into the water? Be careful, the strong currents will sweep you away!' the woman shouted from the shore. Mohanaswamy turned around to see a vague figure of a woman standing there, with a baby on her hip. A small girl was standing next to the woman. The mother and daughter kept waving at him frantically, asking him to come back. They could have been his mother and sister. Then a gigantic wave rose in the sea, sweeping him off his feet and rolling him ashore. He stood up, shaking, and then dragged his feet back towards his hostel.

As he walked past the woman, she started yelling at him. 'It's a full moon night,the sea is in high tide. You people should be more careful!' she shouted. To avoid her, Mohanaswamy lied to her in his broken Hindi, 'Mujhe Kannada nahin aati.'

On his way to the hostel, he made a resolution that he would never behave like a gay thereafter. His gayness was the root cause of all problems. He should do whatever it took to become straight. He would fall in love with a girl and show to the world, especially to Sumit, that he was also capable of making love to a girl. As he came near the Shiva temple, he pronounced that he would never attempt to take his own life again. He also thanked the mother–daughter duo and uttered a prayer for them.

~

Since it was the final year of their engineering course, the students went on an industrial tour starting from Pune and then onwards to Mumbai, Delhi and Goa. On their return journey, the plan was to go on a beach tour in Goa. On the day the students arrived in Goa, they indulged in drinking. Mohanaswamy was surprised to see mutton and wine shops everywhere in the city. The two lecturers who accompanied the students also drank to their heart's content till late night. When they woke up in the morning, it was already past ten. The students got ready to set out on the beach tour. They planned to cover as many beaches as possible and the locals advised them to hire bicycles.

This put Mohanaswamy in a quandary. He did not know cycling. In the small town where he lived, he had always walked to all his destinations. His father had stopped cycling long ago. His sister also had not learnt cycling. Girls never rode a bicycle in that small town. A couple of boys of his age group lent their bicycles to Mohanaswamy and tried to teach him pedalling. But Mohanaswamy had not succeed then. Frustrated, his friends gave up, saying, 'A GanSu can never ride a bicycle.'

The bicycle came to haunt him in Goa that day. All the boys and even the three girls in the group knew cycling. They ridiculed him and laughed at him, who always scored the most in tests. Even the lecturers were upset with him. 'What? You say you don't know cycling? What kind of a boy are you! We can't afford to hire a bus just because you don't to how to ride a bicycle. We will carry on, you can stay back in the hotel,' one of the lecturers said in contempt.

Sitting in the hotel room, Mohanaswamy felt left out. He thought of going out on his own, but then he dropped the idea. It was a low budget hotel situated in the city outskirts. He then thought of going to his hometown, but realized that he did not have enough money. He spent time walking up and down in the hotel corridor and reading periodicals.

He began cursing himself for not learning how to cycle and in his despair, he suddenly began to believe that had he known cycling, he would not have been gay. What else could be the reason? I too have eyes, ears, a nose and a mouth like them. The blood that flows in my veins is as red as theirs. I too have a thinking brain like them. I dress like them. If at all there is a difference between me and them, it is cycling. May be riding a bicycle is a symbol of masculinity. I made a mistake by not learning it as a child. Had I mustered my courage I would have I would be chasing girls. I should learn cycling as early as possible. I should start hankering after pretty girls. All these years, I was searching for the reason behind my plight. Now I have found it. I know the solution.

But who would teach him? He did not have the courage to ask his friends. He would once again become the target of their jokes. What if he went to his hometown? But his father was too old to teach him how. Moreover, other people in the town might laugh at him for learning a basic skill this late in life. I have to learn cycling at any cost. Are there cycling schools on the lines of driving schools? he wondered. But he hadn't seen such schools anywhere. So what to do?

Finally, he wrote to his sister Janaki in Hospet, explaining his enthusiasm to learn cycling. But he did not reveal the intention behind it. 'I feel very tired walking to the college in the sun. So I have to learn cycling,' he explained. By then his relationship with his sister had improved. Though she was the one who christened him as 'GanSu', she had grown up to be more mature. She had developed a love for him over time, having realized that he was a sweet, harmless, studious boy. After he got good ranking in PUC and left for a far-off city for further studies, her affection for him multiplied. She wrote to him every week. When Mohanaswamy was in the fifth semester of his engineering degree, she got married. The groom was from nearby Hospet. When she left for her in-laws' house, she hugged her brother and cried. 'If you have any problem, come to me. I will look after your needs,' she had said, asking him to forgive her follies. 'You haven't done anything wrong, Akka, why are you crying?' he tried to console her while tears welled up in his eyes. It was also possible that she had got a clue about Mohanaswamy's sexual orientation. But she had no courage to ask him directly and neither did he dare tell her openly.

Janaki replied within a week. 'Come over to Hospet. I have made all arrangements for someone to teach you cycling. Dadapeer, the son of Shekhavali, who works in our agriculture fields, will be perfect for the job. He is a good-natured boy. He studies in ninth standard in the government school. He also helps his parents in the fields. He is not so good in studies. But he rides a bicycle well. Not just a bicycle, he even drives his father's tractor. He also repairs his bicycle on his own. Don't feel shy that you will have to learn cycling from a boy much younger to you. I will ask him to take you to scarcely populated places so that you can learn cycling without any hesitation,' she stated in the letter. Tears shone in Mohanaswamy's eyes as he read the letter. He thanked his sister in his mind, packed his things and without caring a hoot for his classes and exams, he left for Hospet. The possibility of him becoming straight had rekindled his enthusiasm.

Dadapeer and Mohanaswamy set out for Hampi, a temple town located within the ruins of Vijayanagara, about eight kilometres away from Hospet. 'Don't worry, brother. It is not difficult at all. You will learn it in half a day,' Dadapeer was assuring him like an older man. The one-rupee tip that Janaki had given to Dadapeer was doing its work.

They reached Hampi by bus and hired a bicycle. There is a huge ground in front of the Pampapati temple. Dadapeer suggested that it was an ideal place to learn cycling. But Mohanaswamy refused to go there, fearing that people may laugh at him. Then they decided to go to the ground in front of Achyutaraya temple at the base of Matanga hill.

Lifting the bicycle in their hands, they took the stairs abutting the hill to reach the temple. Dadapeer told Mohanaswamy to fold his hands before the statue of Nandi. 'If Basavanna is pleased with by your devotion, he will make bicycle learning easy for you,' he said.

Mohanaswamy was puzzled. What is the relation between Nandi bull and bicycle? 'Why do you say so?' he asked Dadapeer.

'That is because Basavanna is Shiva's vehicle,' Dadapeer replied. Without saying anything more, Mohanaswamy folded his hands before the idol.

Dadapeer wore khaki shorts that reached till his knees and a tight-fitting red shirt over it. It was Mohanaswamy's. 'Bring a couple of your old shirts while coming,' Janaki had mentioned in her letter. Although Dadapeer was seven years younger than Mohanaswamy, he had a broader frame. So Mohanaswamy's shirt was tight for him. Even then he had worn it happily. That dark-complexioned boy who showed his white teeth while smiling irked Mohanaswamy. But he could not express his irritation because the right now he was his teacher.

The sprawling ground in front of Achyutaraya temple was deserted. 'I will go for a test ride just to make sure the cycle is in good condition,' Dadapeer said, excited. It took about twenty minutes for him to finish two rounds. 'The cycle is in perfect condition,' he said, after coming back. 'First, you must fold your hands and pray to Mother Earth seeking her pardon,' he ordered Mohanaswamy.

'What sin have I committed to seek her forgiveness?' Mohanaswamy asked.

'All these days she was carrying our weight. Now she has to carry the weight of the cycle too along with our weights. So we are overburdening her,' said Dadapeer.

Since it was no use reasoning out with Dadapeer, Mohanaswamy quietly bowed down, touched the earth and raised the soil to his forehead.

Dadapeer said, 'Brother, before you begin your tryst with the bicycle, you must keep one thing in mind. This thing called the bicycle is very mischievous. If you are scared of it, it will lord over you. If you are bold, it will surrender to you. So pluck up your courage, pray to god and take charge.'

Thus began Mohanaswamy's training. For the first two rounds, Dadapeer came running behind him. He then taught him how to first run along with the cycle and sit on it while maintaining balance. 'This is like the moon catching up with the running clouds!' he explained. His metaphors and similes amused Mohanaswamy and reduced his anxiety. Mohanaswamy fell off the bicycle twice and injured his knees. He applied some dry mud over it. 'Don't worry, brother. Don't feel bad because you are hurt. New skin will grow in its place. It is like putting on new garments while giving up the old and torn ones,' Dadapeer exhorted him. Within half an hour, Mohanaswamy learnt to mount a running cycle. He went for two rounds in the ground. The third round was a breeze.

However, the next round was a disaster. As he pedalled on, two foreign tourists, both men, were coming on two bicycles from the opposite direction. From far they looked like red and blue dots coming in full speed. As they approached closer, Mohanaswamy panicked, lost his courage and the bicycle grew insolent. It refused to listen to Mohanaswamy's commands and prayers and ran into the narrow space between the two riders. As a result all three fell down. 'What man, you don't know cycling?' the men screamed, rising from the ground, dusting off their clothes. They went near Mohanaswamy and asked him, 'Are you okay?'

An anxious Dadapeer came running from behind. He shook their hands and tried to explain the situation in his broken English. 'My brother … cycle … my teaching … he learning.' From their accented English, Mohanaswamy gathered that they were probably Europeans. They found it interesting to see a small boy teaching bicycle to a grown man. They asked Mohanaswamy and Dadapeer to pose for a photo along with their bicycle in the backdrop of the Achyutaraya temple and the alpine scenery of Gandhamadana and Matanga hills. Dadapeer readily agreed, wiping the sweat on his forehead with the sleeve of his shirt and tucking his shirt in. 'You knicker … my knicker … same same … You red shirt … I red shirt … same same,' he told the foreigner who was in shorts and a red shirt. He also pinched him saying 'same pinch'. They liked it. But Mohanaswamy was quite uncomfortable. He was embarrassed that those strangers had now come to know that he was learning how to ride a bicycle this late in life. After the photo session, the two men bid them goodbye and cycled towards the temple, saying that they had to click some more pictures inside.

Though Mohanaswamy wanted to ride a couple of more rounds, it was getting late. Also, he was exhausted and his throat was parched. Dadapeer went off to get some tender coconuts from the vendors near the Vijaya Vitthala temple. He took five rupees from Mohanaswamy and went on the bicycle.

Half an hour went by, but Dadapeer did not return. Mohanaswamy began to panic. A bird cried out hoarsely. The air was filled with the chirping of crickets and humming of mosquitoes. There was the fear of encountering snakes and scorpions. The town was also believed to be haunted by the spirits of the dead. The Gandhamadana hill was not visible now. Even the Matanga hill could not be seen. He wondered if the foreigners were still around and went looking for them, for some company. On entering the precincts of the Achyutaraya temple, he saw their parked bicycles and felt relieved. He groped his way inside, his eyes adapting to the darkness. The moonlight lent him some visibility, but the foreigners were not to be seen around.

Mohanaswamy grew anxious again. Then he heard screams coming from inside. He walked in that direction and approached another stone structure. Inside the temple, he saw two entwined bodies rolling about on the floor, naked. Their clothes were lying near the pillar. Hiding behind the pillar, Mohanaswamy watched the two men making love. This was the first time that he was seeing two men doing it so openly. So far he had only fantasized about it. But now, right in front of his eyes, two male bodies were rolling on the floor, moaning in pleasure. As he looked on, the two men whispered something into each other's ears and laughed. There was no trace of hesitation. Mohanaswamy realized that he was not alone. There were others like him in this world. In the precincts of Achyutaraya temple, Mohanaswamy felt enlightened.

~

When he stepped out of the temple, he ran into Dadapeer, who had four tender coconuts in his hands. 'Where were you, brother? I went to Kamalapur to bring tender coconuts.'

Mohanaswamy gestured with his little finger that he had gone to urinate. 'Thank you very much, Dadapeer, for teaching me how to ride a bicycle.'

'Not a big deal my brother, it's not rocket science,' said Dadapeer, dismissing his praises.

They sipped the tender coconut water after breaking open the shells with sharp stones. As they prepared to go back to Hospet, Mohanaswamy told Dadapeer, 'Let's not go from the side of the temple. We will go in front of the Vijaya Vitthala temple. I know it is a longer route, but we can go chatting on the way, enjoying the cool breeze.'

As they walked down the road pushing the bicycle along, Mohanaswamy thought, not just riding a bicycle, even if I learnt to fly an aeroplane, I will still want to make love to a man and not to a woman. Surely someone somewhere would be there, waiting for me.

KASHIVEERA

Kashiveera was five years older than Mohanaswamy. He was dull in studies but very good at sports. There was a story behind the weird name 'Kashiveera', which his mother Vimalakka once narrated to Mohanaswamy.

That day when Mohanaswamy went to their house, Vimalakka was sorting and cleaning rice, sitting in the front yard. Her husband Bhujang, whom Mohanaswamy addressed as Bhujang uncle, had gone to office. Kashiveera was at the playground. His two sisters had gone to their friend's house. Vimalakka was very fond of Mohanaswamy, he was the apple of her eye. Not just because he was her friend's son, but more importantly, unlike her son Kashiveera, he studied and always got good marks in school. Kashiveera, though older than Mohanaswamy, failed in his exams several times and now he had regressed to Mohanaswamy's class. Her own son's dismal performance notwithstanding, Vimalakka was never envious of Mohanaswamy. She lavished a mother's love on this dimple-chinned, obedient boy.

When Mohanaswamy went to their house, Vimalakka welcomed him and gave him allittu – a delicacy made from cornflour mixed with sugar, ghee and milk. The light of the noonday sun flooded the entire yard, lending plenty of visibility to Vimalakka who was separating out small pebbles from the rice grains. Munching on the allittu balls, Mohanaswamy was trying to swat houseflies that had stormed into the yard. Vimalakka then began narrating the story behind the name 'Kashiveera'.

Vimalakka had two daughters and when she became pregnant for the third time, she was under tremendous pressure. Her husband had threatened that if the third one also turned out to be female, he would drown the baby in a lake.

'Don't worry, this time it will be a boy. Just keep praying to god,' Mohanaswamy's mother would try to console her, but Vimalakka's worries wouldn't go away.

'Last time also I prayed desperately to all the gods, but none of them came to my rescue!' she wailed. Her worries intensified as her pregnancy advanced.

Then came the festival of town deity, Kumaraswamy. The temple was situated atop a hillock. A big fair was held during the month of Shravana every leap year. Since he was the most favoured deity of political leaders, the fair used to be held with much pomp and show. Sadhus from far off places visited the town and stayed there for about two months in anticipation of a handful of alms. During the festival, food was served in the temple and on other days, they went from house to house, seeking alms.

One such sadhu who came to Vimalakka's house one day sensed her anxiety. 'Why, mother, why are you so worried? Pregnant women should not stress so much, it affects the baby inside,' he said.

Moved by the softness in his voice, a depressed Vimalakka collapsed on the threshold, holding the plate of rice in her hand. The sadhu helped her sit up and lent a sympathetic ear to her story.

He came up with a solution to her woes. He said that she should worship the grave of Kashimpeera at the dargah in the town and by doing so she would certainly be blessed with a baby boy.

His words cast a spell on her. She started going to the dargah every day. Once a week, she ate the jaggery served there and poured her heart out to the maulvis who reassured her of the power of prayers.

Well, Kashimpeera did not disappoint her. She was blessed with a son. Bhujang's joy knew no bounds.

But there was ruckus at home on the day of the naming ceremony. When the priest, who was performing the rituals asked Bhujang what name had been decided for the child, Vimalakka instantly said, 'Kashimpeera.'

The priest was stunned. And so was Bhujang.

'Have you gone mad?' he shouted.

But Vimalakka was in no mood to listen to anybody. 'I have already decided this and I will not compromise with any other name,' she said firmly.

Had it been any other day, Bhujang would have slapped her across the face for raising her voice and being adamant. But that day he couldn't as she was a new mother – a mother who had borne him a male child.

Feeling defeated, he requested the priest to name the child as per her suggestion.

'What nonsense?' Now it was the priest's turn to yell. 'Can Brahmins ever give a Muslim name to their children? No, never! At least I cannot be party to such sin,' he said furiously.

The auspicious hour was running out as the tug-of-war over the name continued. Finally, a Kannada scholar present among the guests came up with a solution. Instead of 'Kashimpeera' the name should be 'Kashiveera,' he said, because in Kannada, the syllables 'pa' and 'va' did not make much difference to meaning. This was convincing enough. Everyone agreed to it. Thus, the child was named 'Kashiveera'.

However, Vimalakka continued calling her son 'Kashimpeera'.

Kashiveera was not good in studies. While his sisters passed their exams with flying colours, he flunked every alternative year. He was also a bully and complaints against him reached his parents quite often. But he was good at sports. He had grown up to be a six feet tall, brawny young man by the time he reached class ten. He practised volleyball, day in and day out. Gauging his aptitude, his father decided to put him into sports. Accordingly, Kashiveera underwent training and earned himself several state-level prizes and a solid reputation.

Had it been only this, it would have been a happy story. But it was not to be. Kashiveera picked up many vices as he went from city to city playing volleyball. People at home came to know that he had begun smoking and drinking. His winsome looks earned him many girlfriends by the time he completed his first year in college. He would often roam around with idlers and loafers on his bicycle. His parents tried counselling him, but he refused to listen. 'My own son has gone out of my control. What can I do?' Vimalakka would express her helplessness to Mohanaswamy's mother.

As days passed, Kashiveera's well-built masculine body began to draw Mohanaswamy's attention. By then, Mohanaswamy had found himself a well-paying job in Bengaluru. Whenever he visited his hometown, he would be dying to meet Kashiveera. He would invariably get him some gifts. If anyone mentioned his vices and misdeeds, Mohanaswamy would rush to his defence. 'Don't scold him unnecessarily, Aunty. It is only such bold boys who come up in life, you will see,' he would try to reason with Vimalakka.

Kashiveera sensed Mohanaswamy's adulation for him and began trading with his good nature. He would pester him for money every now and then.

'Don't plunder me to buy cigarettes and alcohol,' Mohanaswamy would admonish Kashiveera affectionately, gently stroking his bulging biceps.

'No … I won't. I have to buy some college books,' Kashiveera would say, flicking back the strands of hair on his forehead and grinning impishly.

Mohanaswamy knew very well that Kashiveera would never complete his graduation. Even then, he continued giving him money for his college books.

In the evenings, he would often go to the playground to see Kashiveera play volleyball. Kashiveera looked handsome in a small vest and a netted baniyan. His strong muscles, robust thighs, hairy armpits, the way he roared while scoring a point during the match, the way he drank water – pouring it into his mouth from above and spilling some on to his chest, the way he put water on his head and shook it from side to side – all this held Mohanaswamy in awe. Kashiveera began appearing in his dreams, naked. He would fantasize about him in different positions.

One day, Mohanaswamy got a chance to touch his body. When he went to Vimalakka's house, none of her children were around. Vimalakka offered him some coffee. 'I have heard that in Bengaluru, vendors sell even dry shit of humans. Is that true?' she started chatting. Bhujang uncle had gone to the weekly shandy and Kashiveera had gone to the saloon for a haircut. The girls were away at a Hanuman temple in the outskirts of the town. As Mohanaswamy prattled away with Vimalakka, Kashiveera came home.

'Amma ... will you pour some water on me?' he shouted from the front yard and walked towards the bathroom.

'These children won't even let me cook in peace! Mohana, can you please go and pour some water on him?' she requested Mohanaswamy.

Mohanaswamy was thrilled at the golden opportunity that landed on his lap. Like a child eager to grab a piece of candy, he scampered to the bathroom. 'Mohana, be careful. See to it that the water from his body doesn't touch you, he has just come back from a saloon. Our Peera is a boor, he has grown like a donkey and has no maturity,' Vimalakka shouted from inside the kitchen.

When Mohanaswamy entered the bathroom, Kashiveera had already removed all his clothes except his briefs and was sitting on his haunches in the bathing yard. Water was boiling in a huge vessel on the hearth in the corner of the bathroom. Kashiveera's body glittered like gold, reflecting the fire in the hearth. A gold chain around his neck glinted in the same light. This was the body that appeared in Mohanaswamy's dreams night after night. Now it was there, right in front of his eyes. Mohanaswamy was mad with happiness and anxiety. With trembling hands, he began lifting the boiling water with a mug from the large vessel, looking at Kashiveera from the corner of his eyes. A clean-shaven Kashiveera looked as handsome as Manmatha – the god of desire. When he yawned and stretched his arms, Mohanaswamy noticed that he had shaved his underarms too. He felt horny as he pictured a shiny shaving blade sliding down Kashiveera's armpits.

Mohanaswamy helped Kashiveera soak his clothes in cold water. Then he began pouring hot water all over his body. 'You went to the saloon, so you should wash yourself properly, each and every part of your body,' he instructed. 'Rub yourself here, rub there,' he went on.

'Enough, Mohana, enough!' Kashiveera interrupted, but Mohanaswamy did not stop. He went on pouring water. Finally, unable to quell his desire, he snatched the soap from Kashiveera's hand and stepped into the bathing yard.

'You don't know how to rub your back, I will do it for you,' he said and began rubbing his back with the soap.

'Why do you want to do it, Mohana? Leave it,' said Kashiveera, sensing something amiss.

The sight of Kashiveera's almost naked body burst Mohanaswamy's dam of restraint and filled him with an overwhelming desire. From his back, Mohanaswamy's fingers moved towards Kashiveera's chest, stomach, feet, legs and thighs. Kashiveera stood still, without reacting. Mohanaswamy had completely lost self-control, as if possessed by some devil. Unmindful of Vimalakka's presence in the kitchen, he then tightly hugged Kashiveera from behind. A fit of hysteria overtook Mohanaswamy and he slowly slid his hand into Kashiveera's underwear.

Mohanaswamy reeled under a strange mix of joy and trepidation. It was a first experience. The feeling was akin to entering the sanctum-sanctorum of the temple and touching the idol inside. Mohanaswamy felt giddy and breathless as he clasped Kashiveera's member in his hand, resting his head against his back. Kashiveera still did not react, quietly sensing Mohanaswamy dominating his body and moaning. But when Mohanaswamy brought his face closer to Kashiveera's face from behind on the pretext of applying soap, Kashiveera couldn't take it any longer.

He turned round and hit Mohanaswamy's face so hard that he fell over on the floor with a loud thud.

'What's that noise?' Vimalakka shouted from the kitchen.

'It's a cat burglar!' Kashiveera shouted back.

Mohanaswamy's clothes had become completely wet. He felt bitter realizing that Kashiveera had no interest in his body. He had fallen in the eyes of Kashiveera. He felt ashamed. He did not dare touch Kashiveera again. Bedraggled and teary-eyed, Mohanaswamy walked out of the bathroom and went home.

The entire day he wallowed in guilt and remorse. Kashiveera is like my elder brother. He calls me 'Mohana' affectionately. I laid my hands on such a righteous person, shame on me. God should punish me for this. I am bad, a petty insect. I am a poisonous snake that bites its caretaker. There is no place for a venomous creature like me on this earth. Why did I desire a man who is five years older than me? I remember Vimalakka telling me that when I was a baby, Kashiveera used to take me on his lap and play with me. How could I forget that? My sinful body that craves men should be cut into pieces and the flesh cast to vultures. I am a pervert. My mind is full of filth. I deserve no respect. I am useless, I am sick!

Bogged down by self-criticism, Mohanaswamy cried for a long time, sitting in front of the idol of Krishna. Unable to show his face to anyone, he walked with his head lowered in shame. He languished in silence.

After a while, his grief subsided, but fear took its place. What if Kashiveera tells my parents? What if he reveals this to Vimalakka and Bhujang uncle? What if people in the town get wind of it? Will they not chase me away and pelt me with stones? They all have known me as an obedient boy and today's episode will lay bare my true persona. No, no, this shouldn't happen. I should go and apologize to Kashiveera. I should assure him that this sinner will never touch him again. 'Kashiveera, please ... please forgive me, just this once,' I must say. The moment he says he has forgiven me, I must pack my bags and leave for Bengaluru. Then I should not see him again. I should be careful that he does not even appear in my dreams.

By evening, Mohanaswamy penned a letter to Kashiveera. In the letter, he berated himself for his vulgarity and coarseness and begged his pardon. 'I don't deserve to be treated like your younger brother,' he wrote. Then he went to the playground and waited for him. As usual, Kashiveera came, jovially chatting with his friends, and played volleyball till darkness fell. Mohanaswamy sat there all the while but did not dare to lift his head and look at him.

After the game was over, Mohanaswamy went and stood in front of Kashiveera with his head bowed. He couldn't look him in the eye. 'I want to speak to you, Kashiveera,' he said hesitatingly.

'What is it?' Kashiveera snapped while putting on his t-shirt.

Mohanaswamy could not utter a response as his heart was thumping in his chest. He quickly handed over the letter to Kashiveera, said sorry, and hurriedly walked out of the playground.

That night he couldn't sleep a wink. He got up from his bed several times, went to the puja room and prayed: 'Lord, please make Kashiveera forgive me, I beg you.'

Next day, he was on his way to a grocery store when Kashiveera came speedily from behind on his bicycle. Mohanaswamy turned around as he heard the screech of tyres. 'Meet me behind the Durgamma temple this afternoon. I want to speak to you,' he said in one breath and whizzed past. Has he forgiven me or not? Mohanaswamy was perplexed. Whatever the case may be, he had to meet him.

He went near the Durgamma temple in the afternoon as instructed. The temple was in the outskirts of the town, situated amidst a tamarind grove. The area was always deserted, especially in the afternoons. People usually went to the temple on Tuesdays and Fridays, mostly in the evenings. When Mohanaswamy went there, Kashiveera had not yet arrived. Mohanaswamy suddenly grew weary. Is this a plot by Kashiveera to get me caught? Whatever I have done, is it wrong in the eyes of the law? Will the newspapers publish stories about my heinous act? I have heard that this is not illegal in America and Europe, but here in India, the police will kick your ass and put you in jail if they get wind of it. If something goes wrong, what will happen to my life? What will my parents do? If my employers come to know that I am such a person, will they not throw me out? What if I don't get any other job? Mohanaswamy began feeling dizzy as he was overcome by countless fears.

Kashiveera came half an hour later. Mohanaswamy stood up, feeling guilty. 'Sit down, sit down,' Kashiveera said and forced him to sit.

Since there was no one around, Mohanaswamy mustered all his courage and said, 'I am sorry, Kashiveera. I made a blunder.'

'Hey, no issues!' Kashiveera cut him short, pulling a pack of cigarettes from his pocket. He put one cigarette between his lips and offered one to Mohanaswamy.

'Do you smoke?'

Mohanaswamy declined the offer.

'Yeah ... I know you don't smoke, you are a good boy. Not a spoiled brat like me. That is why everyone tells me that I should be like you,' he said, grinning mockingly. 'Okay, if you don't smoke, leave it. You can at least light this for me,' he said, holding out the matchbox to him. Mohanaswamy had to strike the match several times as his hands were shaking.

Kashiveera took a deep breath, blew out the smoke and said, yet again with a sarcastic smile, 'I read your letter. Your handwriting is so good, maraaya, not like mine which looks as if a spider has crawled across the page.'

Mohanaswamy was in no mood to laugh. 'Whatever happened that morning, please don't reveal it to anyone, Kashi,' he pleaded again.

'Hey, why are you so scared, maraaya? This is not something uncommon in the world. Don't worry, I won't tell anyone,' Kashiveera said in an assuring tone.

Mohanaswamy finally felt relieved. 'Thanks Kashiveera, you are big-hearted,' he said with gratitude, both hands folded before him.

'Oh that's okay, no issues at all. Perhaps you were overcome with desire, so you touched me, right? So what? Did I get pregnant?' he said, holding his arms suggestively around his belly and laughing loudly at his own joke. Mohanaswamy looked at him helplessly. 'Come on, everyone commits mistakes. So do I. How can I go on and talk about your mistake to your parents or to the people in the town? How can I go and complain to the police? I have even hidden the letter that you gave me so nobody sees it,' Kashiveera said, a nasty smile still playing on his lips.

Mohanaswamy sensed some impending doom and decided to leave the place right away. 'I need to go now, Kashiveera. I will never touch you again,' he said and prepared to go.

Kashiveera stopped him. 'Hey, wait, maaraya, why are you in a hurry? You have neither a wife nor children waiting at home. Wait, I want to talk to you,' he said as he finished smoking his cigarette and threw away the butt. Then he sat on a stone platform and beckoned Mohanaswamy to sit next to him.

A bird shrieked hoarsely in a tamarind tree above, adding to Mohanaswamy's feeling of unease.

'I am in trouble, Mohana. I had taken some money as loan from someone. They have started pestering me to return it. I have already given them all the money that my father had given me to pay fees. Now I am broke. If you give me five hundred rupees, I will pay my college fees and somehow complete my degree this year. Then, like you, I will to take up a job. I know I am very bad in studies, but I still need to make a living. If I am unemployed, no girl will be willing to marry me,' Kashiveera said, pinching Mohanaswamy's thigh.

'I don't have so much money right now,' Mohanaswamy said honestly, rubbing his burning thigh.

'No problem. Give me whatever you have now. The remaining amount you can withdraw from the bank tomorrow and give.'

Mohanaswamy extracted his wallet from his pocket and counted the notes – there were three hundred-rupee notes, one fifty-rupee note, two ten-rupee notes and a two-rupee coin. 'I have only this much,' he said.

'No problem. You can give me the remaining amount tomorrow,' Kashiveera said, grabbing the money.

'I have to leave now,' pleaded Mohanaswamy.

'Okay, okay, go, your mother will be waiting for you,' Kashiveera said, patted his cheeks and saw him off.

When Mohanaswamy had walked a couple of yards, he heard the sound of a woman laughing. The sound was coming from behind the temple. Suspicious, he tiptoed towards the tamarind grove and hid behind the temple wall to see what was happening on the other side. To his surprise, he saw Kashiveera playfully dangling a hundred-rupee note in front of a woman. She was jumping high to catch it, giggling incessantly. Finally, when she managed to snatch the note from him, Kashiveera grabbed her by her waist and pulled her closer. The tamarind grove resonated with the peals of their laughter.

Mohanaswamy couldn't stand there any longer. He felt uneasy thinking that the woman must have come along with Kashiveera much earlier and overheard their conversation. He ran towards his house, his heart pounding with anxiety.

Kashiveera's thirst for money seemed insatiable. It wouldn't stop at five hundred rupees. He started nagging Mohanaswamy every now and then for cash. Mohanaswamy did not have the guts to tell him off. He was too afraid. He stopped going to his hometown, spending even Deepavali holidays in Bengaluru. 'I'm bogged down with work in office. What can I do?' he yelled at his parents when they questioned him.

But Kashiveera wasn't one who would let him get away so easily. He went to Bengaluru and knocked on his door.

'I had gone to your house yesterday. Aunty gave me your address and asked me to see you. She wept a lot, saying that you haven't come home for a long time. You shouldn't cause such grief to your parents, Mohana, it's bad,' he admonished him and managed to wheedle another thousand rupees out of him.

Before leaving, he said, 'You have been giving me so much money, Mohana. I feel this is an unequal exchange. If you want, you can touch me once. I won't mind staying back for an hour.'

Mohanaswamy's blood started boiling. 'You brute … Go, go from here, get lost!' he opened the door and shoved him out. Kashiveera stepped out, laughing and Mohanaswamy banged the door shut behind him.

He thought of changing his residence. But Kashiveera would surely find him there as well, gathering the new address from his parents. So there was no point.

One morning, when he went to office, he was stunned to see Kashiveera there, sitting and chatting with his colleagues. He seemed to have got in their good books with his charm. 'Mohana, your friend is so smart and dynamic!' one of them said, impressed with Kashiveera.

Mohanaswamy took Kashiveera to a nearby restaurant, deciding not to have any conversation in the office. He ordered two cups of coffee. But Kashiveera called the bearer again and asked him to give him a masala dosa first. Then he drew out something from his pocket and held it towards Mohanaswamy. 'Take this … This is laddu from Tirupati. I had gone there for the darshan of the deity and got some prasad for you too. Have some, Mohana. Everything will be fine,' he said. But Mohanaswamy refused to accept the packet. 'Ayyoo ... you can take out your anger on me, but why on Tirupati Thimmappa? What has he done to you? You will land in unnecessary trouble, take it,' he said forcing the packet into his hands.

As Mohanaswamy reluctantly accepted the laddu and began eating it, his eyes fell on the paper in which it was wrapped. It was a photocopy of the letter he had written to Kashiveera. Filled with horror and anguish, he tore the letter into pieces.

'The Lord of Tirupati is very greedy for money. He snatched away all that you had given me. Now I have no money left even to buy a cup of coffee. Give me one thousand rupees,' Kashiveera said, flashing a smile.

'I don't have so much cash. I also have to send some money home,' Mohanaswamy said in disgust.

'How can you say that, Mohana? You have such good friends at office. You can borrow from one of them. I'm sure they won't say no to you,' Kashiveera said. Mohanaswamy took out a thousand-rupee note from his pocket, gave it to him and walked out of the restaurant without saying a word, without even waiting for his coffee. He couldn't concentrate on his work all day. Kashiveera's attractive body, which once turned on his imagination, had now turned nightmarish, haunting him day and night. He dreaded that Kashiveera may suddenly appear before him, anytime, anywhere, asking for money. The sweetness and fondness he had once nurtured for Kashiveera had now turned to fierce hatred. He wanted to share his grief with someone, but whom could he speak to freely?

There were hardships on the home front too. Since Mohanaswamy had stopped sending money home, he had to face several questions. 'It is my hard earned money, I will spend it as I may please. Who are you to question me?' he once said sourly to his mother, leaving her in tears.

She was heartbroken. 'Somebody has done some black magic on my son. He was never like this before,' she went around telling everyone.

His father was furious. 'What do you do with so much money? Have you picked up any bad habits?' he enquired. Fearing his anger, Mohanaswamy borrowed some money from his friends and sent it home.

One day he got a call from his father at eight in the morning. He was calling from an STD booth since there was no phone at home. 'Your mother is suffering from severe stomach pain. Till last night she was fine, she served us dinner and went off to sleep as usual. It suddenly began at two. She couldn't even drink water, the pain was so bad. We rushed her to a hospital.

Doctors said there are stones in the kidney that need to be removed. Come over immediately, Mohana, we need a lot of money for the surgery. You will have to get at least ten thousand rupees in cash,' his father said.

Mohanaswamy's heart melted. 'Don't worry, Appa, I will somehow arrange for the money. Just go by what the doctor says and take care of Amma,' he said, trying to comfort his father. But the harsh reality was that there was no money in his bank account thanks to Kashiveera. He did not feel like asking his friends again, as he had already borrowed quite a lot from them. In the anguish of utter helplessness, Mohanaswamy sought divine mercy and succour. Lord Krishna, save me from this crisis.

Then an idea flashed in his mind. He had a gold chain weighing about twenty grams, gifted by his mother. By pawning it, he could get around ten thousand rupees. Having made his decision, he took a quick bath, packed his clothes in a bag and set out for the pawn shop.

While he was walking near the signal, a hijra came to him, clapping loudly. She caressed his cheeks, cracked her knuckles in front of his face and asked for money. She was a regular at the signal. She once told Mohanaswamy that she hailed from his district. Mohanaswamy had always felt a strange mix of compassion for and fear of her. She would touch men without any fear, caressing their cheeks and shoulders. And if they did not resist, her hands would freely and move on to the other parts of their body. He envied her courage. But he couldn't imagine himself wearing women's clothes like her and roaming on the streets. He knew very well that he wouldn't dare get his dick chopped off. Though he desired men, he loathed dressing like women. During his teenage years, when his friends started teasing him for his feminine traits, he hesitated to talk to them. Once, he had taken part in a tiger dance during the college annual gathering. After the programme was over, everyone made fun of him, calling him 'hennu huli', a female tiger. A Kannada movie by that name had hit the screens just recently. Since then, Mohanaswamy had not taken part in any dance programmes, including his office parties.

Many times he tried to escape from this inner turmoil, but to no avail. I should behave like men, he would tell himself, but his feminine mannerisms would invariably reflect in his behaviour. So he was very particular about what he wore. Colours like pink, red and yellow were a strict no. When it came to sexuality, no female body would attract Mohanaswamy. Once or twice he had tried masturbating, imagining naked women. But he couldn't. No woman, no matter how beautiful, would come in his dreams.

When the hijra insisted for money, he reached into his pocket and searched for change. He got a five-rupee coin, but thought it was a bit too much of an amount to give her. But since he had already taken it out, he gave it away. 'Thanks, brother, I will not ask you for money for the next two-three days,' she said. Then, she blessed him, placing her hands upon his head, 'May all good things happen to my brother. No evil shall befall him.'

Mohanaswamy smiled and said, 'Every time I give you money, you tell the same thing. But my woes have not gone away. I am tired of malicious people.'

'Oh brother, if you want to suffer, people will make you suffer. If you are submissive, they will take advantage of you. But once you rise firmly and put a bold front, they will back off. You must vow to rise from this mire. Every morning when you wake up, put your hand on your chest and say, "I have not done anything wrong". If you are strong, then no one can harm you.' Saying so, she clapped her hands and went looking for another man.

Mohanaswamy went to the pawn broker, pledged his gold chain and got Rs 9,800 as a loan against it. Then he went to his office to apply for leave. There he saw a familiar figure seated on a chair, waiting for him. 'Why Mohana, why are so you late to work today? Are you okay?' Kashiveera enquired, feigning affection. Mohanaswamy's head started reeling as he thought of the fresh notes in his wallet.

Even then, he decided to take Kashiveera to the usual

restaurant as he did not want any scene to be created in the office. They ordered coffee. The restaurant was full. Since the bearers were all busy, the owner himself came with the coffee cups. He was somewhat fond of Mohanaswamy, who was a regular customer. He took special care of him.

'Kashi, please don't trouble me today. I am going home. There is an emergency. Amma is unwell. She has been admitted to the hospital. She has to undergo an emergency surgery today. If you don't believe, look at this luggage,' Mohanaswamy pleaded.

Kashiveera's lips parted in a smile beneath his moustache. 'Mohana, telling a lie isn't easy, especially for good boys like you. Leave it to bad boys like me,' he said saucily. Then he took out a packet from his bag, held it out to Mohanaswamy and said, 'Take this, this is chatnipudi. Your mom asked me to give it to you. Yesterday I had gone to your house,' he said, smiling triumphantly, thinking he had exposed his lie.

Mohanaswamy ran out of patience. 'If you are not ready to believe me, what can I do, Kashi? Yes, till last night she was fine. But she developed a stomach pain early this morning. Appa told me to make arrangements for money and come over immediately. I am broke as I have been giving you so much money. I had to pledge my gold chain in exchange of cash this time, see here!' he said piteously and showed him his wallet.

That was the cue. Kashiveera snatched the purse from him, took out the cash and stuffed the notes into the pocket of his trousers. 'Your father has enough money, Mohana, he will take care of the expenses. You are a young boy, you don't worry.' He returned the empty wallet to him, got up and started walking towards the exit.

It took Mohanaswamy a while to understand what was happening. He felt a sudden surge of anger. He ran behind Kashiveera, who had reached the main door. Mohanaswamy grabbed his legs from behind and pulled him with full force. Kashiveera fell down with a thud and bumped his forehead. He uttered a frightful howl. But Mohanaswamy was not in a position to listen to his cries. He threw himself on him and pulled out the notes from his pocket. Kashiveera managed to rise, but seeing Mohanaswamy furious, he did not dare hit him back.

Mohanaswamy had lost his mind and began yelling, 'You scoundrel, you are taking away my hard earned money! Are you blackmailing me? Who are you? What have I done to you? Why are you troubling me like this? Yes, you once looked handsome in my eyes. Yes, I felt like touching you. I felt like kissing you. I felt like sleeping with you. I felt like sucking your penis. I felt like getting fucked by you. Is that wrong? Well, when I realized that you were not interested, I did not touch you after that, not even your fingernail. You want to tell this all to the people in the town? Go ahead and tell them. Tell the whole world! Tell all these people sitting in the restaurant here. You can even go and tell the police. What can you take away from me? Mind you, from now on, if you ever come to me again, asking for money, I will finish you.' His whole body was shivering with rage, his eyes red with anger.

Kashiveera stood still seeing this enraged avatar of Mohanaswamy. All the people in the restaurant looked on in stunned silence. Then abashed, ashamed and wincing with pain, Kashiveera wriggled out of the place.

Trying to compose himself, Mohanaswamy trudged wearily back to his table. He was surprised at how he was unravelling in full public view. His coffee had become cold and flies were floating on it. He looked around to find the people still watching him. He was just about to go, when the restaurant owner came and placed a small plate containing the bill on the table. The bill was eight rupees. Mohanaswamy put a ten-rupee note on the plate, looked up at his face and said with a feeble smile, 'You can keep the change.'

But the man did not smile back. He drew out a two-rupee coin from his pocket and put it back on the plate. Then he spoke in a serious tone, 'Don't come to our restaurant from tomorrow. This is a place where decent people come. You should go find another place.' Saying this, he walked back to the cash counter.

Mohanaswamy was flabbergasted. I will have to face and fight people like Kashiveera all through my life. Otherwise, I just can't survive on this earth. As this depressing thought came across his mind, he sank in his seat. Then, lifting himself heavily, he walked slowly towards the exit.

ANAGHA – THE SINLESS

It was five in the morning on a chilly Dhanurmasa day. The biting cold had left even non-living things shivering. Kalleshi was up much before his grandmother called out to him. In fact, he hadn't slept the whole night. He switched on the light.

'Have you woken up?' His granny shrieked from her bed.

'Yes, Ajji,' he said and the old woman slipped back into her sleep.

But it wasn't his fast-approaching preparatory examination that was on Kalleshi's mind. He gently closed the door of the room. Without wearing his chappals, he tiptoed towards the back door and opened it. He had oiled its hinges the previous night so the door opened easily without squeaking. His father was not home and that gave him courage. After his mother's death, his father hardly slept at home. If he found out where his son was going, he would surely beat him to death.

After coming out of the house, Kalleshi strode briskly towards the Soogam well. He would have ran if it weren't for the dogs that would chase him. The well was in the outskirts of the town, not very far from his house. On reaching the place, he heaved a sigh of relief as Somanna had not yet arrived. He was in town for sure, because Kalleshi had seen him the previous evening, fishing out a pot that had fallen into the well. This being Dhanurmasa, Somanna would definitely come to the well at the crack of dawn for a bath.

Kalleshi hid behind a neem tree. The soft light of dawn had pleasantly lit the area. After a while, a figure loomed at the end of the road. A dog barked in that direction. The figure threw a stone at the dog and it ran for its life, letting out a shriek. It was Somanna, no doubt. Kalleshi's heart began pounding at the sight of the man he was waiting for with bated breath.

First, Somanna took off the towel from his shoulder and spread it on the stone platform abutting the well. He stood on it, raised his arms towards the sky, joined his palms together, closed his eyes and offered prayers.

Then, braving the biting cold, he removed his shirt and dhoti and threw them on the floor.

Kalleshi swallowed his saliva as he saw Somanna in the buff, except for a langoti. Kalleshi's body turned hot like a metal rod on fire. But on the inside, he was shivering and began grinding his teeth. He felt like a butterfly hovering over a flower. He hugged the tree tightly, desire flaring in his eyes as he watched Somanna exercise rigorously.

Somanna was so strong he might have had the capacity of enjoying a body massage from an elephant. His python-like muscles ran up and down his well-built body during his workout. When he did push-ups, the bracelet on his forearm touched the ground every time with a 'thunn...' sound, breaking the silence of the atmosphere in a rhythmic pattern.

Unable to suppress his desire, Kalleshi came out from behind the tree and walked towards him. 'Somanna...' he whispered. Somanna was surprised to see Kalleshi in front of him, appearing from nowhere. He would have snapped at Kalleshi reflexively, but bit his tongue and smiled upon hearing the tenderness in his voice.

Quite breathless with excitement, Kalleshi put his quivering finger upon a bead of sweat on Somanna's bare midriff just above his navel and burst it. He looked up at Somanna's face, which still wore the smile. His silence encouraged him. Leaning forward and standing on tiptoe, Kalleshi caressed Somanna's face, feeling the hot breath under his nose. His hands then strayed to his neck, arms, chest, nipples and stomach. He sat down on his haunches at Somanna's feet. From there he lifted himself slowly, his fingers lightly tracing Somanna's skin from his toes to his thighs.

There was no resistance.

Finally, mustering all his courage, Kalleshi slid his hand inside Somanna's langoti and clasped his genitals firmly.

And that was it!

Somanna slapped him across his face so hard, that Kalleshi collapsed to the ground. 'Bosudike!' Somanna screamed, kicking him madly, treating him like a stray dog.

Kalleshi tumbled down, screeching 'Please stop!'

'Thooo!' Somanna spat in his face. He then removed his langoti, flung it on the heap of clothes and dived into the well.

It took a while for Kalleshi to recover from the blow. He touched his cheeks wincing in pain. He rose with difficulty, holding on to his smarting waist. Dragging his feet towards the well, he peeped inside. There was no sight of Somanna, he could only see ripples and hear the sound of water splashing.

He walked towards the heap of Somanna's clothes, picked up the langoti and sniffed it rigorously, getting intoxicated by the scent. Driven by unbridled desire, he pressed it on all parts of his body and finally slid it inside his shorts, wrapping it around himself. Next, he found a beedi pack and a matchbox in Somanna's shirt pocket. He lit up a beedi, drew a deep puff and blew the smoke out. Then he threw the still-burning matchstick on Somanna's clothes and walked home.

The flames rose, roaring towards the sky as Somanna continued swimming.

~

There was an old, dilapidated well in the backyard of Kalleshi's house. A few years ago, people in the neighbourhood used to get water from it. But after Kalleshi's mother fell into the well and died, everyone, including Kalleshi's family stopped using it. The water in the ninety-feet-deep well had turned green and filthy. A few fish and a couple of tortoises, which had existed in the well earlier, were long dead. Now there were only long worms feeding on the algae and snakes feeding on rodents. Bats hovered above the area in the evenings.

But that day, even the animals were frightened as the well reverberated with Kalleshi's piteous screams. 'I am sorry, Appa! I will not do it again, Appa!' Kalleshi was begging pathetically, hanging upside down by a rope, six feet above the green water in the well. 'Appa, I am scared, please pull me up, I beg you!' he screamed as he heard the rustling of animals inside. 'Ajji, save me! Please!' But there were no replies to his desperate pleas. 'Amma…!' he called out to his dead mother as he felt breathless from the pressure of the rope tied around his legs and chest.

But there was no one around to pay heed to his pleas. After fastening the rope to a tree trunk outside the well, his father Veerabhadrappa had gone and sat under a neem tree at a distance, casually smoking a beedi. His grandmother was sitting in the kitchen and sobbing helplessly, pleading for Kalleshi's rescue, but it fell on deaf ears. She even tried to pull the rope herself with her feeble hands but couldn't move it even an inch.

Tears lurked beneath Veerabhadrappa's fiery red eyes as he sat unmoved, not uttering a word. He had slept at Sunanda's house in Koodligi the night before. Since it was a Monday, he had left early in the morning, and had gone to Balaswamy Betta to offer puja to the god on top of the hill before returning to the town.

'What Veeranna … I heard your son Kalleshi laid hands on Somanna's balls?' an acquaintance, whom he met on the way, had jeered. Those searing words were still ringing in his ears.

Kalleshi grew despondent after pleading continuously.

His heart sank and his mouth dried up. Suddenly a bat flapped its wings over his face with a squeaking sound. Kalleshi's heart missed a beat and he urinated in his terror. The fluid ran down over his shirt and then on his face before the drops spattered on a pair of snakes copulating down below. They hissed in anger for being disturbed and that was the last thing Kalleshi remembered before he passed out.

~

It was late evening and the oil lamp placed in a niche on the front wall of Sangamma's house was burning dimly. As a custom, the man who came before others would blow it out and step inside the house. As Sangamma closed the door behind her, the extinguished lamp outside indicated that she was engaged with a client. This was to avoid other men coming and knocking on the door when she was sleeping with one man.

Sangamma was very choosy and particular about her clients. She took time before converting acquaintances into bed partners. For the first few days, she would engage the man in informal conversation and only when she was convinced of his trustworthiness, she allowed him into her bedroom.

But that night it was almost time to sleep and nobody had come yet. A disappointed Sangamma was cursing her luck just when she saw a figure walking towards her house. Finally there was someone.

It was Veerabhadrappa.

He must have got tired of that Koodligi Sunandamma, that's why, she thought to herself bitterly. But as Veerabhadra came nearer, she saw another man with him. 'I won't sleep with two men, they cannot force me,' she muttered. But when they were at the door, she realized it was Kalleshi, his son. The rumours she had heard about him in the morning came to her mind and she sensed that something was amiss.

'Blow out the lamp,' Veerabhadrappa told his son.

Kalleshi breathed out through his mouth feebly and the fire flickered weakly for a beat and burnt steadily.

'Oye ... Blow it out properly, with force!' Veerabhadrappa commanded impatiently.

Scared stiff, Kalleshi blew it out, exerting all his strength.

'Veeranna, after sleeping with the father, I can't sleep with the son,' Sangamma said without mincing her words.

Veerabhadrappa did not answer immediately. Instead, he extracted two betel leaves from his pocket. He kept some areca nut pieces and two hundred-rupee notes on the leaves, asking Kalleshi to hand over the tambula offering to Sangamma.

'Sangamma, I can understand your dilemma. But I am not asking you to sleep with him. By now you must have come to know about the deeds of this son of a bitch. This morning's episode has torn me apart. Just do me a favour. Take him inside and check if he is a man or not. Just think you are treating him clinically, nothing else. Kindly do it for my sake,' he begged her with his hands clasped.

His distressing pleas and the currency notes in Kalleshi's hands swayed Sangamma. She held Kalleshi's hand to take him inside but Kalleshi tried to escape.

'Oye … bosudike … go inside, go!' Veerabhadrappa commanded, hitting him on his head.

Kalleshi helplessly followed Sangamma into the room. Sangamma closed the door behind her. Veerabhadrappa sat in a corner of the front yard, anxiously puffing at a beedi.

The door opened within a few minutes. Sangamma came out. She had taken her blouse off and wrapped her sari across her chest.

'What happened?' Veerabhadrappa's eyes burnt with anticipation.

'Kaamanna – the god of lust – hasn't favoured your son,' she sighed.

Veerabhadrappa drew one last puff and squashed the butt of his beedi on the cow dung plastered floor. Pushing

Sangamma aside, he barged into the room. Kalleshi was curled in a foetal position, holding his clothes tightly to his chest. The sight of a nude woman had left him feeling nothing but fear and disgust. Veerabhadrappa didn't say a word. He just went up to his son and began kicking him with all the energy he could muster. He trampled him like an elephant crushing ants under its feet.

'Don't beat me, don't ... I beg you ... Leave me!' Kalleshi begged pathetically, doubling up with pain.

Fearing the boy might die, Sangamma pushed Veerabhadrappa aside and threw herself on Kalleshi, holding him tight and shielding him from his father's blows. 'Please don't beat him, don't ... Please!' She wailed.

But Veerabhadrappa was in no mood to heed her words. He continued kicking him and amidst the blows, she also got hurt.

'Stop it, Veeranna, this is god's creation! Don't insult god's creation,' she shouted furiously.

Veerabhadrappa stopped. Throwing a contemptuous glance at Sangamma, he said, 'I have kept five women like you. But I fail to understand why god gave an impotent son to a powerful man like me.' He spat on the floor. 'From today on, this impotent creature is not my son, nor am I his father!' He picked up his towel from the floor, dusted it off, put it on his shoulders and walked out in a huff.

Sangamma followed him to the door. 'Veeranna…' she called. Veerabhadrappa stopped and turned around. Looking into his eyes she said, 'I will tell you one thing, remember it well. Unlike you, your son hasn't committed the sin of keeping five women and pushing his wife into the well. Every Monday, you go to the temple and offer puja, but even the god you worship loathes women, mind you! He likes only men!'

'Bevarsi, rande!' Veerabhadrappa's eyes splashed with malice as he spat expletives at her and walked away.

Sangamma wore her blouse, went inside the kitchen and brought a glass of water. She helped Kalleshi sit up and made him drink it. He put on his clothes in front of her. When he lost his balance while sliding his trembling legs into his underwear, Sangamma held his hand and supported him.

'Going ahead, life will be very difficult, my child. People don't respect impotent people and prostitutes,' she said sadly.

'But I am not impotent,' Kalleshi said dolefuly.

He dragged his feet towards the door, limping. Sangamma watched him walking in the opposite direction of his house. Then, remembering something, she went inside and brought the hundred-rupee notes given by Veerabhadrappa. 'Kallesheee!' she hollered, hurriedly walking towards him. She slipped the currency notes into his palm and said, 'Be happy, wherever you go.'

Kalleshi melted into the darkness.

Sangamma brought out a matchbox and lit the lamp placed in the niche in the front wall of the house.

AT THE PEAK, FOR THE FIRST TIME

Mohanaswamy's flight was to take off from Bengaluru at 9.30 a.m. The airport was a two-hour drive from his house. But he hadn't booked a taxi. He had decided to take a bus as the frequency of BTS buses to the airport was quite good. He was going to Delhi only for a day, and had no luggage except a laptop bag. The taxi fare would have been an unnecessary expense to his company. They had arranged to send him to Delhi to train his co-workers.

It was already half past seven and he was still at home. Domestic check-in wouldn't take much time, but he wanted to leave early so he would reach the airport with at least half an hour to spare.

Karthik had gone in for a bath and hadn't come out yet. He had a habit of spending long hours in the bathroom. Mohanaswamy often objected to it. 'What is the use of pouring water continuously over the body like this?' But Karthik never paid any heed to his grumblings.

'Come out fast, Karthi, I have to leave. I'm already very late!' Mohanaswamy knocked on the bathroom door. How could he leave home before Karthik came out? Who would latch the door from the inside?

Mohanaswamy had woken up early in the morning and got completely ready for his trip. He went over the PowerPoint presentation he had made for the training session. He ironed his clothes. Brought milk from the shop and had his morning coffee. He also cooked sambar for Karthik's dinner. He had a bath at six and Karthik was still sleeping.

Every morning, Karthik invariably woke up late. Mohanaswamy had to shake him and call him three-four times. He sometimes became anxious that in his absence, Karthik may not wake up at all and end up being terribly late for everything. He slept like Kumbhakarna, the demon. 'You have no sense of responsibility. I alone have to worry about everything!' Mohanaswamy yelled at him all the time. Karthik usually responded to this with a laugh. And if Mohanaswamy continued to berate him, he would stride up to him, take him in a tight embrace and seal his mouth with a hot, voluptuous kiss.

The same thing happened today. When Karthik came out of the bathroom, wrapped in a red turkey towel, the scent of Pears soap blended with hot steam wafting from his body, it was already 7.40 a.m. Mohanaswamy, all set to leave, dressed crisply in his business suit, was waiting for him anxiously. 'What is this, Karthi, don't you know I am already late? Even today you took so long. What if I miss my flight?' Mohanaswamy went on heatedly.

Without replying, Karthik grasped him from behind and began kissing his neck and cheeks passionately. 'No, Karthi, no … my ironed clothes will become wet…' Mohanaswamy pleaded. Karthik only got more worked up. He pinioned Mohanaswamy against the wall, kissing his neck vigorously. Mohanaswamy could no longer resist and he gave in, moaning with pleasure.

Releasing Mohanaswamy from his tight embrace a while later, a smiling Karthik wrapped his towel around his waist again and sat on the bed with his legs stretched. He buried his head in a newspaper, expecting a stream of expletives from Mohanaswamy.

Mohanaswamy looked at his watch. It was already 8 a.m. His neatly-ironed clothes were now all damp and crumpled. He did not have another pair of ironed clothes to wear. 'Karthi, what is this? What will I do now?' he cried in frustration. Karthik did not respond, his head still buried in the newspaper. 'Speak up now, say something!' A livid Mohanaswamy screamed, snatching the newspaper away from him.

'Well, why did you wait for me till I finished my bath? If you had left while I was inside, all this wouldn't have happened, right?' Karthik asked, still smiling.

'Then who would bolt the door from inside? What if thieves broke in?'

'Now, don't cook up excuses! What is there in this house that will interest thieves? No gold, no silver, no cash, nothing. Some clothes and a few utensils is all that we have. I know you were searching for a pretext to stay back. You couldn't have left without having a cuddle huddle with me, right?'

'Idiot!' shrieked Mohanaswamy, and picked a pillow from his bed and began swatting Karthik with it. Karthik faced the blows and broke into a fit of giggles.

After a few minutes, Karthik stopped laughing and became serious. 'It's time for you to start now, Mohana, hurry up. Or else you will really miss the flight,' he said. 'Now it's not me who is stopping you.'

His serious tone brought Mohanaswamy back to his senses. 'What clothes will I wear, Karthi?' he cried.

'You can put on my clothes.' Karthik suggested.

'Your clothes will be big for me. How will I wear them?'

'Nothing will happen if you put them on for a day. Please don't make an issue out of every damn thing!'

Left with no other choice, Mohanaswamy walked across to Karthik's room and was shocked to see the main door of the house wide open. 'Oh my god, oh my god!' Mohanaswamy let out a yelp as he ran back into the room and climbed onto the bed, his body shivering.

'What happened, my dear, why are you screaming?' asked Karthik pulling Mohanaswamy towards him.

'Karthi, the door is wide open. We didn't realize it…' Mohanaswamy said in a trembling voice.

For Karthik it was no big deal. 'So what if the door is open? Why are you so worried?' he tried to console him.

'What if someone had come inside and seen us together?'

'Let them see. Nothing is going to happen.'

'You are being so naive, Karthi, you don't realize the gravity of the situation. If someone sees us together and tips our landlord off, we will be kicked out.'

'Nonsense! Besides, we can always look for another house. Why should we be so scared? Have we murdered anybody? We just love each other. It's as simple as that!'

'I am not in a mood to joke, Karthi. My heart is pounding with anxiety. This is illegal. We will be dragged to the police station and put in jail…'

Mohanaswamy was petrified. Karthik pulled him even closer. 'So far nobody has seen us together, right? Don't worry. One day or the other we will have to reveal all this to the world, Mohana … You must pluck up your courage…' Karthik whispered in his ears, trying to comfort him.

'No, Karthi, no. Even if I die, I won't disclose this to anyone. This matter should not go beyond the four walls of the house, it should be strictly between you and me. Otherwise people will not keep quiet. They will chase us to our deaths,' Mohanaswamy said anxiously.

Karthik did not want to drag the matter further. 'All right, forget about it now. Why talk of unpleasant things? You are late for your flight. Wear my shirt and trousers. I will drop you to the airport on my bike,' he said.

Mohanaswamy got up reluctantly. 'I don't think I can catch the flight. It's very late now…'

'If you miss the flight, you can catch the next one. Come on, we'll figure something out.'

Karthik called up the airport and gathered that Mohanaswamy's plane was delayed by an hour. If the technical error was not rectified within an hour, the passengers would be taken in another plane. He got into a t-shirt and three-quarter pants and waited for Mohanaswamy.

Mohanaswamy came out in Karthik's clothes which were a little loose on him. 'Is it okay?' he asked coyly.

'Super...' Karthik gestured with his fingers. 'You look smart!' he said, walking up to Mohanaswamy.

Sensing an impending danger, Mohanaswamy immediately jumped back and wailed, 'Oye, oye, oye! Now don't start all over again...'

Karthik smiled and said, 'You think I don't have any other work? Come here, I will do your tie neatly.' He went near him, removed the tie clip, held it between his teeth, took off the tie, perfected the knot and fastened back the clip in the right place. 'Now you look smarter, Mohana,' he said, pecking him on the forehead. 'Also, your flight is late by an hour. So you can reach the airport without any tension,' he said.

'Really?' Mohanaswamy said in disbelief. Karthik nodded. Mohanaswamy's heart brimmed over with love and affection for him. 'You don't have to come all the way to drop me, then. I will take the bus. Or else you will be late for office,' he said, stepping out of the house with his laptop bag. Going down the stairs, he suddenly remembered something and called out, 'There is sambar in the fridge. And some curd. You only have to cook some rice for yourself for dinner. Don't go to the mess to eat. They add soda to rice – it causes acidity. I may be late at night. Don't wait for me. I will eat something in my flight.' He sprinted down the steps and ran towards the bus stop.

~

Mohanaswamy didn't get a bus as conveniently as he had expected. He decided to wait for ten more minutes at the bus stop and if no buses came, he would take a taxi. He sat down on a bench and looked around. There was a scooter garage beside the bus stop and Mohanaswamy simply could not take his eyes off from the sight that greeted him there.

A brawny young man in a t-shirt was repairing a scooter, squatting on the floor with his back towards the bus stop. His massive biceps stuck out of the short sleeves. He had a tightly-tied amulet around his right upper arm and as he was winding up some scooter parts with a spanner, a bracelet on his wrist rolled over his popping veins, glinting in the sun. As he went about his work, his short t-shirt rode up and his jeans lowered, revealing his ample behind. His butt crack was visible and seeing that the man was not wearing underwear, Mohanaswamy went weak in the knees.

Earlier, Mohanaswamy would fear that if he looked at other men with lust, Karthik would be upset. But now he knew Karthik well – whenever he came across beautiful women, he stared at them without blinking.

Sometimes after coming back from work, hovering around Mohanaswamy while he cooked a meal in the kitchen, Karthik raved about some woman he had met that day. Mohanaswamy objected to this in mock anger as he knew that it was his longing for women that made Karthik even more desirable.

The young man, busy repairing the scooter, suddenly turned around and caught Mohanaswamy staring at him. He pulled his pants up even as Mohanaswamy turned his face away. His heart began panting wildly as he realized he was caught.

'Laay … gandoo…' the man said out loud. Mohanaswamy kept a straight face and pretended the words were not directed at him. Some people waiting for the bus turned in the direction of the voice. However, the man did not leave it at that. 'Laay … gandoo … You … a chakka, a hijra in suit and shoes … You son of a…' he screamed. People began looking at Mohanaswamy.

Backed into a corner, Mohanaswamy turned to the young man and stuttered, 'What … What have I done? Why are you shouting?'

The man stepped towards Mohanaswamy with the spanner in his hand, spewing rage and venom. 'You asshole … eyeing my ass, huh? Come here … I will screw you with some engine oil … Laay … Suvvar … Come here, swine … I will ram my cock up your ass and down your throat ... You motherfucker ... My cock is so big ... You want to see it? Come I will show you...' The man brazenly slid his left forearm into the spanner hole and suggestively moved the tool back and forth over it with swift strokes, yelling mockingly.

Overcome with shame, Mohanaswamy reeled at the blatant insult. Everyone began scrutinizing him as they slowly understood what was going on. A few exchanged jeering glances. By then a bus came by. Mohanaswamy ran and got on the bus without even bothering to check where it was heading to. Luckily, the bus was almost empty and he quickly occupied a seat. Overwhelmed with humiliation, he rested his head against the glass window and sobbed.

The bus started immediately. The man's harsh words rang incessantly in Mohanaswamy's ears: 'Laay ... suvvar ... Come here, swine ... I will ram my cock up your ass ... You motherfucker...' His obscene posture and gestures, the jeering glances of the bystanders, their denigrating laughter – the entire scene filled his vision and began haunting him.

'Ticket, ticket...' came the conductor's voice, but when he saw Mohanaswamy weeping, he guessed something was wrong and retreated hastily, deciding to come back later.

As Mohanaswamy sat in the airport lounge, awaiting boarding announcement, Karthik called him up.

Since both incoming and outgoing calls were charged, he disconnected the call and went to an STD booth at the lounge and called Karthik from there. There was one more reason why Mohanaswamy preferred to make calls from the STD booth. He worried about the prospect of people overhearing him on mobile. But Karthik had no such reservations. He had whispered 'I love you' to Mohanaswamy even over his office phone many times. But Mohanaswamy knew he would not dare do a thing like that in any public space even in his wildest dreams.

When Karthik heard a meek 'hello', he sensed all was not well. 'What happened, Mohana? Is anything wrong?' he asked with concern. His soothing words deepened Mohanaswamy's sadness, but he held his tears back. When Karthik did not hear anything from him, he stayed silent as well. He could guess what must have gone wrong, for this was not for the first time something like this had happened.

'Mohana, did anyone insult you?' he asked softly.

'Yes…' whimpered Mohanaswamy, wiping his nose with his handkerchief.

Karthik sighed. 'Why do you do such things in the public, Mohana? Don't you know that straight men don't like it? They get angry.'

'Tell me, what do I do? Sometimes I cannot just control myself!' Mohanaswamy said helplessly.

A silence descended on them. They could hear each other breathing. After a while Karthik broke the silence. 'Ignore it … Just don't bother … You must learn to get over such things. If you keep brooding over it, you alone will suffer. Nothing will happen to them. Do you understand?'

Mohanaswamy nodded his head.

'Do you understand?' he asked again.

'Yes…' Mohanaswamy groaned.

'Now forget all that has happened and go board your plane. Cheer up … the sky has not fallen on your head! Smile!'

Mohanaswamy smiled with a lot of difficulty.

'Did you smile?' inquired Karthik.

'Yes, I smiled. How can I give you any proof of that over the phone? Can you see me?' Mohanaswamy said with rekindled enthusiasm.

'Don't worry, technology will soon come up with exciting solutions to this problem as well. Today I read a tech article in office … they say that soon a day will come when cellphones will have a TV-like screen where we will be able to see each other even as we talk.'

'Bullshit! That's impossible! How can a mobile phone hold a TV screen? Then phones will become so huge, we will have to carry them on our heads!' Mohanaswamy dismissed the possibility.

'But you never know ... they are coming out with such fascinating things these days that tomorrow even if they say you can have sex over phone, I will believe it!' Karthik said with a laugh.

Mohanaswamy also laughed and said, 'Then I think we'll have to use virtual condoms.'

'Oh, yes, you're right. Or else e-virus will attack.'

Both of them felt light-hearted. Mohanaswamy heard the boarding announcement. He hung up the phone and proceeded towards the gate.

~

'I hoped that things would fall in line once the private airlines became operational. But it's been five years since then and the fate of the private carriers is no different! Except for these new, young stewardesses they have hired, everything else remains the same stale, old stuff!' Mohanaswamy heard a passenger say bitterly. The plane was quite empty. Mohanaswamy sat down on an aisle seat of the right row. He avoided the window seat since he found it scary to look down through the glass. His eyes wandered towards a man in a light brown shirt, sitting on the other end. He must be in his fifties, Mohanaswamy thought, he looks worried.

Mohanaswamy, who always liked to be friendly with co-passengers, said hello to the man and tried to draw his attention. But the man, absorbed in his thoughts, did not turn to him. Not wanting to disturb him again, Mohanaswamy fastened his seat belt and sat reading a Kannada book. Meanwhile, the pilot apologized for the delay and then went about flight safety procedures.

Though Mohanaswamy was quite a frequent flier, he listened to the instructions with utmost attention each time he travelled and followed them religiously. So much so that even if he had already fastened his seat belt, upon hearing the instructions he would loosen it a bit and secure it again.

Mohanaswamy noticed that the man in the light brown shirt had not secured the belt. He still seemed quite preoccupied. Right then a young air hostess strode past Mohanaswamy's seat. He thought of bringing the matter to her notice and said hello to her, inadvertently touching her waist. The woman was beside herself with rage. 'How dare you touch me?' she lashed out. 'You are not supposed to do this. If you want something, you should just call me.'

Those who heard her shouting, stared at Mohanaswamy, who was nonplussed by this unexpected backlash. 'I'm sorry, I didn't do it with any wrong intention. It was just that ... I ... I mean the man sitting over there was not wearing his seat belt, so I thought of...' he tried to explain.

But the woman was in no mood to listen. 'All bloody men are the same. They just need some pretence to paw women!' she said with a scowl and walked off in a huff.

'Enjoy, my son ... nothing will happen,' a middle-aged Sardarji sitting behind him said with a wink.

Mohanaswamy didn't know whether to laugh or cry. How she had reduced him to a teenage boy – eager to touch girls on some pretext! Should he thank her for this or should he reprimand her? He was quite amused. Meanwhile, the man in light brown shirt sitting in the other row put his seat belt on and gestured thankfully at Mohanaswamy with a thumbs-up. Mohanaswamy also flashed a smile at him. The entire episode had lightened his spirits. The flight proceeded towards the runway. Mohanaswamy settled in, deeply absorbed in his book.

A while later, passengers were notified that they could unfasten their seat belts. Mohanaswamy rose from his seat and went to the lavatory. As he bent to wash his hands at the basin, he yelped involuntarily. 'Hey...' he screamed as, for a fraction of a second, he thought he saw Karthik's reflection in the mirror. Then suddenly it dawned on him that it was not Karthik, but himself in Karthik's clothes. Mohanaswamy smiled at his folly. He straightened his loose shirt and came out. Then another inadvertent incident took place.

An air hostess was moving backwards, pulling the drinks trolley along. She accidentally bumped into him, her hips thudding against his waist. 'Oh! I am sorry,' she said coyly, turning around. It was the same woman who had shouted at him earlier.

Now it was Mohanaswamy's turn to show his anger. 'How can you touch me like that? It really irritates…' he yelled.

Her face fell. 'I am so sorry,' she apologized again. Mohanaswamy found it funny, but he continued to put on an angry face. He then walked to his seat, his mind soaring lightly like a kite.

Upon returning to his seat, Mohanaswamy saw that the man in the light brown shirt was sitting on the window seat beside his, and was flipping through his Kannada book. When he saw Mohanaswamy, he placed the book back on the seat and rose to leave. 'No problem, you can sit here,' Mohanaswamy said in Kannada and sat down.

'I love books in Kannada. Earlier I used to read a lot. But now my bank job takes away all my time. It has been years since I read a book. It's rare to see someone reading a Kannada book on a Delhi-bound plane. So I got curious and came here to see what book it is…' the man explained.

'I am Mohanaswamy.'

'I am Ramesh … Ramesh Jamadagni. I work for the Canara Bank.'

'I tried to speak to you sometime back. But you seemed lost. I did not want to disturb you,' said Mohanaswamy.

The man's face turned pale. 'Yes, I met somebody just before boarding the plane. My mind has been disturbed since then,' he said in a dull voice.

'Oh … sorry,' said Mohanaswamy, not wanting to rake up his personal issue further.

'Will you not ask me who it was?' Ramesh implored.

'Oh … Please tell me if you feel like…' said Mohanaswamy, a little perplexed now.

The man looked out of the window and began telling his story without turning to look at Mohanaswamy.

'Her name is Smitha. She was my MCom classmate in Mysore. We were in love. For two years, not a single day went by without us seeing each other. Even though we studied in the same college, we used to write love letters to each other every day. I still have those letters with me. I have kept them in my bank locker to hide them from my wife. Twenty-five long years have passed since we broke apart. Today, I ran into her at the airport. I thought I would never encounter her again in my life.'

'You said you were in love. Then why didn't you marry each other?'

'I did not have the courage, you see, I was a timid man then. We are Brahmins, you know … Madhwa community…'

'Oh…?'

'My parents are very orthodox. They rigidly follow all the customs and traditions of the community. And my Smitha is a Kodava – they eat pork. I knew my parents would not accept her. So I did not even tell them. She insisted that we elope and get married. But I could not muster the courage to run away from home. I did not have a job then. In any case, I realized that this relationship would not last. So, I distanced myself from her. I stopped writing to her, I stopped meeting her. Until then, there were no places we hadn't gone together, no words that we hadn't spoken and no movies that we hadn't seen. Come rainy season, we would go to Shivanasamudra and sit watching the gushing waterfall for hours on end, holding hands. You can imagine how it must have felt when such an intense relationship ended so abruptly. She implored, she begged, she cried her heart out. But I did not relent. Tired, she finally married someone else and moved elsewhere. I too married another girl of my parents' choice. Thus we killed ourselves, sort of.'

'What did she say when she met you today?'

'Nothing. Her anger hasn't died down even after twenty-five years. I wouldn't have minded if she had slapped me across my face in front of everybody. But what hurt me more was that she just ignored me. "I don't know who you are", she said right to my face and walked off.'

'Your physical appearance may have changed over so many years, right? She may not have recognized you.'

'We were madly in love for all those years, Mr Mohan, so how is it possible that we couldn't have recognized each other?'

'I am sorry. I believe you are in a lot of pain.'

'More than the pain, I am racked with immense guilt. I cannot wriggle out of this guilt all my life. I know I betrayed her, I misused her trust. In whom can I confide the agony of my feelings?' he sighed.

'That means, you two were in a physical relation as well?'

The question left Ramesh stumped. 'No, no, no … nothing of that sort. We both came from respectable families. We did not commit any such mistakes…'

'Oh, I'm sorry…' Mohanaswamy said.

Meantime, the stewardess came pushing the trolley of drinks. Ramesh picked up a can of beer. Mohanaswamy went for an orange juice.

'You don't drink?' Ramesh asked.

'No, I don't. I'm not used to it…' Mohanaswamy tilted his head coyly.

'Oh, you're such a gentleman!' Ramesh said with a laugh. Sipping his beer, he lapsed into a deep thought. Mohanaswamy went back to his book.

After a few minutes, Ramesh suddenly turned to Mohanaswamy and asked, 'Mr Mohan, what about you? Are you in love? I mean … I suppose … you are not married yet?'

Mohanaswamy's throat felt parched, he had not quite expected this question. He looked at Ramesh's face for a while and asserted, 'Yes, I am in love.'

'May I know the name of the lucky girl?'

'Kaar…thi…kaa,' he said, drawling out the syllables, so that it sounded like a girl's name. He did not want to tell a complete lie.

'Sweet name,' Ramesh said.

'Thanks,' said Mohanaswamy and smiled. You don't have a car, you have only thikaa, bum … but you are still called Karthika, Mohanaswamy would often tease Karthik.

'For how long have you been together?'

'Um … it's been five years now.'

'Where did you meet her first?'

'We met in a train. Both our reservations were termed RA/C, which meant that we had to share a berth during the entire journey. This first acquaintance eventually turned into love.'

The memory of that first meeting, a night's train journey suddenly heated up Mohanaswamy's body. How easily Karthik had accepted him on such a short acquaintance and made love to him that night!

'Oh! So romantic! Have you informed your parents?'

'Yeah … we introduced ourselves to each other's parents in just three months.'

Karthik had taken him to his town within three months of their friendship and introduced him to his father and mother. 'Please … let's not sleep together in one room, it unnecessarily gives way to suspicion,' Mohanaswamy had pleaded, but Karthik would not listen. That night, Karthik copulated with him in the room, without making noise. Karthik's parents had taken a liking to Mohanaswamy for his modesty and unassuming mannerisms.

'That means they have accepted you?'

'Certainly … his parents are very fond of me.'

'How lucky! Then you must be seeing each other often.'

'Uh huh … we roam around a lot on my bike. She loves riding pillion with me. During weekends, she insists we go out. We keep going to different places – like Mysore, Beluru-Halebidu, Ooty and so on – Karthika doesn't like to stay back in Bengaluru during weekends.'

'That means ... you both stay in the same room in the hotel?' Ramesh asked nervously.

'Of course, yes. How can we, being lovers, stay in separate rooms?' said Mohanaswamy with a laugh.

Will Karthik ever agree to it? Never.

'That means, physical relation between you two ... sorry, don't misunderstand me for asking this,' Ramesh said hesitantly.

Mohanaswamy laughed again. Now he had began to enjoy spinning these yarns. 'Yeah ... In fact, she is keener on it than me. If we don't do it at least twice a week, she will not be happy.'

Not twice a week, Karthi's libido is so high, he wants it twice a day.

'Oh! But being older, I have some advice for you. Please be very careful to avoid untoward events. Life is very unpredictable, you never know what course it will take next,' Ramesh said.

'I keep telling her the same thing, but she is stubborn. She is not in favour of using condoms. She says condoms reduce pleasure.'

Will Karthi ever agree to buy a condom? No, never. We have never bought one.

'Is she careful at least?'

'She tells me nothing will happen to her and not to worry.'

And what can happen to Karthik? Mohanaswamy smiled as he visualized Karthik carrying around a full-blown pregnant belly!

'Even then, please be careful.'

'Yeah … thanks.'

'Where does she stay? Close to your house?'

'No, no … We stay in the same house. Living together.'

'Oh my god … nobody raises any objection?'

'No … in fact her parents are happy with it. They only advise us to avoid bickering with one another and live amicably.'

'What about the landlord who has let out the house to you?'

'Oh … My landlord's family is very fond of us. They sometimes even give us homemade sweet dishes.'

'I did not know that Bengaluru has moved so forward … I used to read in newspapers, but somehow never believed it.'

'Do you see anything wrong in this?'

'No, no … absolutely not … I can understand … But still my advice to you both is, please get married soon. It is not good to stay unmarried for long.'

'But we have never thought of marriage!'

Ramesh was stumped once again. 'Are you serious?'

'To be honest, it is only pleasure that is on our minds

right now. We don't want to take the hassle of getting married and raising kids.'

'Don't say that. There's so much pleasure in family life as well. You must not deprive yourselves of it.'

'Okay, let's see. May your blessings be on me.'

'In fact, I can personally come over and assist you in your wedding preparations. Just give me a call,' he said enthusiastically.

'Many thanks, sir. I will definitely call you when the time comes.'

Ramesh pondered over what Mohanaswamy had said and found it incredulous. How different are the ways of the younger generation! Though I was deeply in love with Smitha, it took me one long year to be bold enough to kiss her. But these youngsters! They have the courage of their conviction.

Mohanaswamy immersed himself in his Kannada book again. His heart was overflowing with inexpressible joy. It had been a great pleasure to be able to converse about his love life and fantasies with someone – though a stranger – during this journey.

After lunch, Ramesh mentioned Karthika yet again. 'Mr Mohan, if you don't mind, can I see her photo? From what you have told me about her, she seems to be a bold girl. I am curious to see how she looks. You must be carrying her photo in your wallet.'

This caught Mohanaswamy unawares. Soon he would have to face the consequences of fabricating so many lies! Nevertheless, he gathered courage and decided to handle the situation cleverly.

'I don't keep her photos in my wallet,' he said, even though two copies of Karthik's photo were always there in his wallet. 'She doesn't like it. She tells me, "I should be in your heart and not in your wallet."'

'Oh!' Ramesh was disappointed.

Mohanaswamy felt sorry for puncturing the man's excitement and decided to come out with another lie. He probably had photographs of some woman in his laptop. One of them could surely pass off for Karthika.

'Oh … I forgot … I have her photo in my laptop. I will show you,' he said.

'Oh, superb! Please do,' Ramesh insisted.

'Just give me five minutes.'

He retrieved his laptop case from the locker overhead and went and sat on another seat to avoid Ramesh's gaze. He shuffled through the image files but they were full of his and Karthik's pictures, taken from their digital camera at different locations. Then there were posters of handsome film heroes from Bollywood movies – Akshay Kumar in *Dhadkan*, Hrithik Roshan in *Kahon Naa… Pyaar Hai*, Salman Khan in *Hum Dil De Chuke Sanam* and the debutant Kannada hero Sudeep in *Sparsh*. Not a single photo of a woman. Finally, he spotted a girl in a photo which had been clicked when Karthik and he had gone for a trek.

Karthik had a craze for trekking, but Mohanaswamy never really enjoyed it. Once, after coming back from a trek to Kumaraparvatha, he had developed an excruciating pain in his legs. Karthik had tenderly kneaded his legs to relieve the pain.

A couple of girls had taken part in the trek, whose names Mohanaswamy had now forgotten. He saw them in the pictures – in which Karthik was also present – one girl was taller than him and another one matched his height. Mohanaswamy decided to present her as Karthika. He went back to his seat and held out the laptop to Ramesh. 'Here you go…'

'Fantastic selection,' said Ramesh, placing his fingers on the girl's image. Mohanaswamy realized that he was making an oblique reference to her breasts. The girl was full-bosomed – but Mohanaswamy noticed it only now.

He had never taken a close look at her during the tour. Instead, he had found her boyfriend attractive – a tall and handsome chap. Mohanaswamy had strongly felt an urge to pull his long straight nose. He even had an earful from Karthik for stealing a glance at him.

'Well, anyway, get married soon,' said Ramesh. He reclined in his seat and dozed off. Mohanaswamy tried to read his book for ten more minutes but soon he too fell asleep.

~

A while later, Mohanaswamy woke up to an ear-splitting sound. The aircraft was making a thundering noise. He saw the crew rushing to the cabin. 'What happened?' a passenger asked an air hostess nervously. Without replying, she walked away hurriedly. A passenger ran behind her but when the plane started tilting to the right, he lost his balance and fell on the aisle. Suitcases began tumbling out of the overhead lockers. Ramesh too woke up to the commotion.

'What happened?' he asked Mohanaswamy.

'I don't know,' said Mohanaswamy anxiously.

A frightened child let out a shrill cry. His mother too began weeping loudly. Passengers were thrown into utter panic when they saw an air hostess coming out of the cabin crying. Someone stopped her and shouted, 'What happened? Please tell us.'

'Some problem in the engine,' she uttered and ran into the kitchen.

Extreme turbulence struck the plane. Someone began reciting religious verses aloud. Some passengers began vomiting and soon the foul smell enveloped the entire plane.

A petrified Mohanaswamy looked out of the window. Delhi's cityscape looked vivid. He lost his nerve when he saw one of the wings almost touching a house as the plane began its descent tilting violently. 'Over, Karthik, over, it's all over,' Mohanaswamy wailed as the fear of death hovered before his eyes. He prayed to god even as more and more bags were thrown out of the cabinets. 'Fire!' someone shouted. Some began slamming at the window panes. 'Please don't do that ... Please!' someone else screeched. Mohanaswamy raised his hands to cover his ears and muttered a prayer – taught by his father in his childhood, his eyes shut and face frozen in dread.

When the airplane crash-landed at the Delhi airport, Mohanaswamy experienced a back-breaking pain. He looked to his side and found Ramesh in an unconscious state. The plane had overshot the length of the runway and had ran into a muddy ground. It rammed against a huge tree with a thunderous sound. A massive fire broke out.

Not many survived the accident. Those seated in the front rows were charred beyond recognition. The pilot, co-pilot, some of the cabin crew and over forty passengers had lost their lives. Some had suffered multiple fractures and others sustained burn injuries. Mercifully, the few passengers sitting in the back rows survived. Mohanaswamy and Ramesh were among the lucky ones. Mohanaswamy's hair was burnt. Ramesh had lost consciousness.

Both the dead and the living were shifted to hospitals on stretchers. Mohanaswamy was examined for over three hours. He felt too weak to reply to queries of the nurses. He had lost the energy to even phone Karthik. When journalists surrounded him and began shooting questions, his temper ran high and he lashed out at them impatiently.

By evening, Mohanaswamy was discharged. A colleague from his office waited for him outside the hospital. Upon learning about the crash, Karthik had called up Mohanaswamy's office in panic. They assured him that Mohanaswamy was safe and that they would pick him up from the hospital. Karthik had tried to get in touch with Mohanaswamy but to no avail. Before leaving the hospital, Mohanaswamy realized that his laptop was missing. But he did not bother to trace it. All that he wanted to do was to cry out aloud. But he could not even do that.

When Mohanaswamy was about to get into the car, he saw Ramesh near a taxi. The warm red glow of the setting sun had spread everywhere. 'I will be back in a moment,' he told his colleague and walked slowly towards Ramesh. They hugged. 'We survived, Mr Mohan, we survived,' Ramesh cried.

Before seeing him off, Mohanaswamy had to confess. 'Sir, I need to apologize to you.'

Ramesh was clueless. 'What for?'

'Whatever I told you during the journey was a lie, an outright lie. Karthika is not my girlfriend. I am gay. Karthik is my partner. We are in a live-in relationship. I was never attracted to girls in my life. It is just that … I just tried to pull a fast one with you. Forgive me for that. I think that's why god punished me like this,' he said.

Ramesh was silent for a while. Then, pulling himself together, he patted Mohanaswamy on his back and said, 'No problem. It's all right. You have not committed any blunder for which you have to apologize.'

WHEN UNSPOKEN WORDS COME BACK HAUNTING

Mohanaswamy's father, Subbaraya, had been ill for quite a while. Whenever he rang home, his mother, Subhadramma sounded worried. Mohanaswamy was aware that he would lose his father shortly. Every time the phone rang, his heart missed a beat in anticipation of the bad news. To save himself from anxiety, he would call his mother several times a day and ask about his father's health. 'Nothing will happen, Amma, don't worry, everything will be all right', he would try to console her even though he knew that his father's days were numbered.

Last night his mother had called after midnight. 'His condition is critical, Mohana. He is struggling to say something but due to severe chest congestion, I can only hear a deep wheezing, gurgling sound. He is continuously shedding tears in helplessness. I think his time is approaching. You come over immediately!'

'Okay, Amma, I will start right now,' he assured her.

But right at that time, Mohanaswamy was caught in a strange dilemma. He had been chatting with a handsome youth, Derrick, for the past few days. That night they had both agreed to meet up at Mohanaswamy's house and Derrick had come over.

Mohanaswamy had got used to his loneliness after his long-term relationship with Karthik ended on a bitter note. After going through the emotional trauma of betrayal and separation, he had been avoiding binding relationships, though in his heart of hearts he yearned for a single, committed, sensitive companion – a soulmate.

Whenever he came across a handsome young youth, he opted to engage in a one-night stand or a fling that lasted a little longer than that. If he liked a man, he would go out with him once or twice. If there was mutual consent, they would hook up for a quickie – just a 'Grr, hrr, thank you, sir' kind – no strings attached. These amatory exploits were fun while they lasted. But they were not meant to be enduring. A few days would pass by and then the hunt for a new date would begin. Presently this was Mohanaswamy's way of life.

Even then, there would be times when, after dating a man, he would think of him as an ideal partner and build castles in the air, visualizing a lifetime bond with him. But the bubble would soon burst as his dream partner would start turning down his requests for meetings, or he would be spotted on some street with his wife and children, or he would have put up a new boy's photo on his Facebook profile. And then it would all be over, with a bitter conviction that loneliness was his true companion. 'This is life, only this much,' he would tell himself. 'I should not desire for more. Desire is the root cause of pain.' But then, if you have to suppress even the smallest of your desires, what kind of life are you living?

Mohanaswamy was getting on in years, facial wrinkles and a few strands of grey hair were beginning to show. Now, after crossing thirty-five, it was quite embarrassing to invite young men over for sex – a half an hour play in bed would drain him out. It was humiliating, shameful. But how could he rein in his inner desires? The more he tried to suppress, the more they re-emerged. Bodily compulsions would break his resolve. All his college friends were married by now, had kids, built houses and were busy working towards securing their future. Mohanaswamy had no such needs and compulsions.

Whenever he went to the bank to open fixed deposits, he would be in a quandary as to whom to appoint as a nominee. His parents were in their twilight years, it would be a foolish thing to nominate them. Once, he wrote the name of Lord Thimmappa of Tirupati in the nomination column. Maybe after my death, the bank officials will put the money in the temple hundi, he thought. And the very thought brought a smile to his lips. When the bank clerk read the god's name against the column, he burst into laughter and showed it to his colleagues. They all laughed loudly and Mohanaswamy joined them, smiling nervously. But then he hurriedly stepped out of the bank to save himself from further embarrassment.

Fear of the future periodically shook him. Who would take care of him if he fell ill? He grew more vigilant about his health and went for regular check-ups, shelling out huge amounts of money in big corporate hospitals. He would anxiously go through the medical reports and thank his stars. 'No, nothing ... nothing has happened to me,' he would reassure himself, heaving a big sigh of relief. And life would go on.

A thought occurred to him quite often. How beautiful life would be had my parents married me off to a good-looking youth at the right age! Then he could have also tied the nuptial knot in front of hundreds of people, seeking their blessings. He would have walked freely into the bedroom on the first night with his life partner, without hesitation, without guilt. He would have led a happy, normal life just like others. Who said the ultimate purpose of marriage is to beget children? Who set these selfish rules that the child has to be a biological offspring? For a happy, peaceful life, a human being needs another human being as a companion. Isn't it as simple as that?

Even when he copulated with Derrick, he was under no illusions that their companionship would be long-lasting. When the stylish young man with his slender, toned body swept him off his feet, Mohanaswamy secretly wished it would last forever. Yet when his fingers traced the youthful contours of that lean body, his mind told him, this pleasure is momentary. These moments are fleeting. When his aging body squirmed in pleasure under Derrick's youthful charms, when his love bites gave him pleasurable pain, Mohanaswamy was ashamed of himself for his perceived inability to give him the same joy in return.

Besides, the very act of sleeping with a stranger gave rise to fear and shame. However, it was always a new body that gave more happiness than a familiar one. How fast it all happened in Derrick's case! Just exchanging a couple of messages on mobile phones, sharing some pictures on the internet and suddenly they were beside each other in bed. It simply proved the Sanskrit adage '*Kamaturanam Na Bhayam Na Lajja*' – those overpowered by carnal desire have no fear, no shame – to be true.

~

Derrick was very reserved, he didn't talk much. Assuming him to be a Christian, and assuming that all Christians spoke English, Mohanaswamy began speaking to him in English. But Derrick faltered and soon lapsed into the vernacular. Mohanaswamy did not find it proper to shoot questions at him about his background, his native place, caste, creed, job and other things. After all, it was their first meeting. They could learn more about each other in subsequent meetings. They took off their clothes in frenetic zeal and stood stark naked in front of each other.

'Shall I remove this janivara too?' Mohanaswamy asked him, pointing to the sacred thread he had worn across his left shoulder and waist.

'No, no need. It won't come in the way,' Derrick said, smiling charmingly underneath his pencil moustache.

It was past midnight when they lay exhausted after devouring each other's bodies. A post-coital shower with Derrick was on Mohanaswamy mind, but Derrick showed no such inclination, saying he was very tired. He soon fell asleep. Mohanaswamy walked to the bathroom alone, turned the shower on and enjoyed a long, relaxing hot water bath, humming his favourite Kannada songs.

When he emerged from the bathroom, wiping himself with a towel, Derrick was not there on the bed. 'Derrick...' he called out. There was no reply. 'Derrick ... Derrick,' Mohanaswamy called out several times, with a suspicion sneaking into him that something was wrong. The man was not to be seen around. He rushed to check in the other bathroom. He wasn't there either. Startled, Mohanaswamy opened the main door. It was dark outside. Derrick's bike, which he had parked in front of the house, was not there. His shoes were missing. He thought of calling Derrick's number and rushed back to his room only to discover that his own mobile phone was missing! He tried his mobile number from the landline and received a switched-off message. He had not memorized Derrick's number, he had only saved it on his cellphone.

Exhausted, Mohanaswamy slumped onto the sofa. There, he was in for another shock – he noticed that the iPad that he had kept on the coffee table was no longer there. He instantly rose, went inside the bedroom and opened the cupboard. There were condoms inside the drawer but all his cash, around thirty thousand rupees and his credit card was missing. He recalled taking out condoms from there and slipping one on himself and one on Derrick.

That bastard must have seen the cash inside when I opened the drawer, Mohanaswamy thought. 'Son of a bitch, he has looted me!' he screamed, took the towel off his waist and flung it on the floor. He staggered into his bedroom and plopped himself on the bed, with his face buried in the pillow. It smelled of Derrick. Mohanaswamy went berserk. 'Idiot, idiot!' he cried out, repeatedly swatting the pillow on the bed.

He could feel his temples throbbing with anger. He thought of calling the police. But they would ask for details. He toyed with the idea of informing his friends. But they were probably busy with their families. They would at the most show sympathy. Worse, they would laugh at him. Mohanaswamy swallowed his pain in silence. He made his bed and he lay on it.

Right then the landline phone rang. He jumped off the bed, and picked up the receiver. 'Derrick!' he cried.

'It's me, your mother, Mohana ... I have been trying your mobile for quite some time, but I am getting a switched off message.' Subhadramma was on the line.

'What happened, Amma, why are you calling so late?' he asked impatiently.

'Mohana, your father's condition is very serious. He is trying to speak but phlegm is choking him, he is unable to utter a single word...' she continued.

Mohanaswamy was completely frazzled as he sat on the bus. He had had a tough time registering a complaint about his lost credit card. The girl on the line asked him his card details before registering the complaint. But all the details were saved on his iPad which Derrick had stolen. He had to ferret out a heap of old receipts and invoices. By the time he was done with the procedure, he was completely worn out. Luckily, Derrick hadn't used his card. Then, he had to inform his office about his missing iPad. The cost was to be borne by him. While money wasn't a big issue, loss of data was. To cap it all, his colleagues had bombarded him with scores of questions.

Mohanaswamy was exasperated. In exchange of a few hours of pleasure, he got more than he had bargained for. He resolved not to bring strangers home again. Booking a room in a hotel seemed the best bet, even if it meant paying good money for it. But then again, that could be even more scandalous because he had heard that some hotels installed CCTV cameras in rooms. Then, what options were left?

His mother was calling him every hour. 'I think your father's death is approaching. He is still weeping. He is worried about you, that you are not married yet,' she said over the phone, crying miserably.

Mohanaswamy was at his wits' end. What is weighing on my mind the most? Is it my father's imminent death or the loss of my iPad and other valuables? It is better if my ailing father passes away. It will be a big relief. As these ignoble thoughts came to his mind, Mohanaswamy was consumed with guilt and shame.

Of late, his relation with his father had gone cold. But as a child he had been very attached to his father. He would look forward to playing with him as soon as he came back from work. Sometimes his father would take him to the Sunday shandy. Perched high on his shoulders Mohanaswamy would feel on top of the world. During Deepawali, he would go to the market with his father to buy crackers. It was fun bursting them early morning on Naraka Chaturdashi. Both father and son would go to the barber shop together. Sitting on chairs next to each other, they would look at each other in the multiple mirrors on the walls. In some mirror, their eyes would meet and his father would wink at him with a smile. That would make little Mohanaswamy blush.

Mohanaswamy was very proud when he passed his pre-university exams with flying colours. He went around town with his head held high as people heaped praises on him. His joy knew no bounds when he got a seat in a reputed government engineering college in Bengaluru.

But that had somehow not really pleased his father, who seemed to be in a dull mood. One day, he summoned him to the backyard of the house. 'With my meagre salary, I can't look after your expenses in a city like Bengaluru. I also have the responsibility of marrying off your sister. You know everything,' he said, wringing his hands.

Mohanaswamy was moved. 'Don't worry, Appa, I will take care of my fees and other expenses. I will find some job and work my way through college…' he assured him. Thereafter he never asked his father for money. He worked as a newspaper vendor in the morning and as a waiter in a hotel in the evening. There were embarrassing moments when he had to throw newspapers at the doorstep of some of his classmates, or when he had to serve tea and snacks to girls from his college who came to the restaurant where he worked. But Mohanaswamy did not lose heart. He paddled his own canoe and never went cap in hand to anyone, including his parents. Now he was proud about hard work. His efforts had paid dividends. He repaid his education loan within just three years of taking up a job. Money was no longer an issue for him.

But what hurt him was his father's indifference towards him. He noticed that he and his father were drifting apart. When he went home during holidays, his father wouldn't talk to him with the same love and affection. He wouldn't take him to market. When guests came home, he avoided introducing him to them. Appa had changed. But Amma had not. She was the same doting mother, who seemed to have quite forgotten that her son was an adult and not a child any longer. He missed her when he was in Bengaluru but when he went home he sometimes felt suffocated by her smothering love. After he finished his engineering degree and got a job, she was after him to get married. 'Why do you say no to marriage? What is wrong with you?' she cried. Then she would seek divine intervention by performing some puja or the other. On somebody's advice she even performed Srinivasa Kalyana, the wedding ritual of Lord Thimmappa, for eleven consecutive weeks. But even that did not help as her adamant son stuck to his guns. 'This Lord Thimmappa is shameless. He will get married any number of times but has no concern for my son!' she would shower curses on her god.

After he started getting a big, fat pay cheque at the end of each month, he tried giving money to his father whenever he went home. His father hesitated to even touch it. 'Give it to your mother, I don't want it,' he would say. But his mother would take the money. She would proudly tell her friends about it.

Although Subhadramma loved her son a lot, it was difficult for her to understand his sensibilities. It was only Mohanaswamy's father who could faintly discern his behaviour which he found to be very different from the boys of his age. Subbaraya used to read *The Hindu* newspaper everyday and had become familiar with terms like 'gay' and 'homosexual'. Once or twice he had even discussed the matter indirectly with his colleagues. Though his son had not revealed it, he doubted whether his Mohana's temperament was akin to what he had read in the newspapers. He had noticed that Mohanaswamy took more interest in feminine tasks. He would keenly draw rangoli designs in the veranda during Sankranthi festival. Like his sister, he loved applying mehendi on his palms. Initially, Subbaraya dismissed all these as childhood tendencies which he assumed would fizzle out as his son grew up. But once, when Mohanaswamy was in college, he saw him secretively wearing his sister's bangles, and sensed that somewhere something was seriously wrong.

Subbaraya was under the impression that people called 'gays' were a group of perverts living in far-off big cities like Mumbai or Kolkata. So he was scandalized when a thing called homosexuality came knocking on the doors of his orthodox family. He didn't have the nerve to ask his son directly. He couldn't share it even with his friends and colleagues. Whenever the topic of homosexuality came up for discussion at his office, he would be all ears. 'Such things happen if parents don't raise their children properly. A father should realize that just sowing a seed is not enough. He should also know how to raise the tree,' a colleague had once remarked. His words pierced Subbaraya like a sword and left him wallowing in guilt. Where did I go wrong in bringing up my son? he would often ask himself.

An incident had taken place during Mohanaswamy's high school days that worsened his father's worries. There was a well in the backyard of their house. Subbaraya used to bathe by the well every morning. He would remove all his clothes except his striped briefs, draw water from the well by lowering a pot into it and pour water over his body. After his bath, he would wipe himself with a towel and wrap it around his waist, while sliding his underwear off. Then he would wash the underwear on the raised stone platform, spread it out to dry and then go inside the house.

While Subbaraya religiously washed himself every morning by the well, what he did not notice initially was a pair of small eyes watching him all along. The moment he started pouring water over himself, Mohanaswamy would run up to the terrace, taking the stairs. 'Why do you run so fast? What's the hurry? Go slowly!' he had chided the boy a couple of times. But when it became a daily affair, he was perplexed. 'Why are you running to the terrace now?' he asked but did not get any convincing answer. He grew suspicious and started watching him closely. What was little Mohanaswamy up to? To his horror, Subbaraya realized that his son ran to the terrace to catch a glimpse of his nude body.

The truth was not only saddening, it was nauseating. The next time he saw Mohanaswamy running to the terrace, he upbraided him, 'Oye, Mohana, why are you going up the terrace? Come down. Go inside and study.' He gave him a beating and after that, Mohanaswamy did not go to the terrace when his father was bathing.

As Mohanaswamy grew up, Subbaraya realized that overall, his son's gait, body language, tone of speech and behaviour matched what was written in the newspapers about gays. And this realization was a bitter pill to swallow.

His worst fears came true following another ugly event. They lived a small house. There were no separate rooms for parents and children. They all slept in the middle yard – Mother, Father, Mohanaswamy and his sister Janaki, all next to each other – spreading mattresses on the floor. The parents would wait till late night for the children to fall asleep so that they could have their moments of intimacy. As time passed, even the parents lost the interest and patience to wait till the children slept. They would doze off along with children.

Once, in his sleep, Subbaraya felt a hand clasping his private organ. Assuming it to be his wife, he stretched his arms towards her. But she was in deep sleep and was quite irritated to be disturbed. 'Take your hands off, it is so humid! Why don't you simply go off to sleep?' she snapped and turned to the other side. Subbaraya was confused. But when the same incident repeated itself the following nights, he grew suspicious and turned to look at Mohanaswamy, sleeping next to him. He shook him in an attempt to wake him up, but Mohanaswamy did not open his eyes. You can't wake a person who is pretending to be asleep. Subbaraya was shocked. Unable to stomach his son's behaviour, he sat up, put both his hands on his face and wept silently.

He did not mention the incident to his wife because he knew it was of no use, she simply wouldn't understand. But he brought about a change in the sleeping arrangement. He told her, 'Our children are growing up. From today onwards let them sleep in the other corner, a little away from us.'

She resisted the idea. 'Why? They are still small, let them sleep near us, else they will get scared,' she said.

But Subbaraya was firm in his decision. There on, the children started sleeping away from their parents. Mohanaswamy sensed the motive behind his father's decision and became very careful with him henceforth.

After Subbaraya understood his son's sexual orientation, he hesitated to scold or beat him. An incident that had taken place in his childhood was etched in his memory. Subbaraya had a friend named Thippeswamy, a jovial and clever boy, very popular in class. But he died when they were in tenth standard. The image of his body floating in a well and his father sitting and sobbing still hovered before Subbaraya's eyes. Only two days before that, Subbaraya and his friends had gone to the temple fair in town. The main attraction at the fair was the sight of beautiful girls roaming around coyly. Thippeswamy had joined his friends, but unlike them, he wasn't staring at girls or raving about them. Subbaraya had noticed it. He also noticed that Thippeswamy look for excuses to touch him unnecessarily. But he ignored it.

Suddenly there was commotion at the fair. Rudre Gowda, son of a leader of the town, was found slapping Thippeswamy across the face, left and right, holding him by the collar.

'I am sorry, I am sorry, leave me!' Thippeswamy was pleading.

A furious Rudre Gowda continued bashing him and pushed him to the floor.

'What happened, what happened?' the boys asked Thippeswamy, anxiously flocking around him. But the boy did not utter a word and went home crying.

Rudre Gowda wouldn't leave it at that, given the age-old acrimony between his and Thippeswamy's families. The next morning he went and stood in front of their house, yelling at the top of his voice. A big crowd gathered as Rudre Gowda hurled a stream of expletives at Thippeswamy's father. 'What is this? What kind of a son have you fathered? Yesterday, during the fair he pawed my cock and pulled it. Is he a man, or something else? Do one thing, just wrap him in a sari and make him a jogati, a eunuch!' he shouted, spitting on the ground. Then, with a wicked smile on his face, he narrated the whole incident to the curious onlookers.

Thippeswamy's father was suffused with crippling shame. He dragged his petrified son to the front of the crowd and asked furiously, 'Did you do that? Did you really do that? Tell me!'

'Sorry, Appa, I am sorry. I won't do it again!' Thippeswamy cried miserably. His father whipped him black and blue with a twig of a tamarind tree. Thippeswamy's teary eyes searched for his friend Subbaraya in the crowd and they held a desperate plea to save him. That piteous scene remained etched on Subbaraya's mind. Finally, an elderly person saved Thippeswamy from his father.

The next morning, Thippeswamy's body, covered with bruises, was found floating in the well. 'It's only natural for a father to punish his son who commits a mistake. Why did the boy take such an extreme step?' people discussed, blaming the victim.

Rudre Gowda also came to see the body. 'If young boys tread the wrong path, it is the duty of us elders to correct them. How could I simply keep quiet?' he went on telling people, defending himself.

As a young boy, Subbaraya couldn't fully comprehend his friend Thippeswamy's behaviour. But things became clearer after he observed similar traits in his son Mohanaswamy. In fact, when he looked into his son's eyes, he saw Thippeswamy there. He resisted scolding or beating him. At the same time, he lost all his affection for him. One day, he broached the matter with his wife.

'Somehow, I feel Mohana's growth is not happening the way it should be,' he said in a low tone. He knew that his wife would not be familiar with words like 'gay' and 'homosexual', so he tried to put it as sensitively as possible.

'Why do you say that? What is wrong with our Mohanaswamy? He has grown so big and hefty.'

'No, no … not that,' Subbaraya stuttered. 'I think he is not growing into a man in the proper sense. Maybe he will not be in a position to get married,' he added hesitatingly.

Subhadramma hit back savagely, 'Are you in your

senses? Do you know what you are saying? How can you say such things about your own son?' She began sobbing.

Subbaraya grew weary. 'Why do you cry over each and every damn thing? I just told you what I feel. If you don't want to believe it, don't!' He walked angrily towards the backyard.

Subhadramma went to the backyard, stood in front of her husband and said firmly, 'I have always worshipped god with utter devotion and sincerity. God cannot deceive me like this.'

Though Subhadramma spoke firmly to her husband, she was also aware that everything wasn't normal. She recalled how her son, till recently, used to bring water from the tap, holding the pot against his waist like girls. She told him several times to carry it on his shoulders like boys, but he would not listen. He had no interest in spinning tops and playing marbles with the boys of his age. Instead, he loved weaving wire baskets, often snatching one from his mother. Once, when he was in the second year of his engineering course, his mother had seen him standing in front of the mirror and painting his lips red with a paste of vermilion and oil. She was taken aback. Of late, she had been hearing snide remarks about her son from women in the town who were curious to know why he was not getting married.

About two or three years after taking up a job in

Bengaluru, Mohanaswamy had come home. That night, after savouring home food to his heart's content, he went to bed and was soon snoring softly. This time, his mother, determined to test his virility, went and sat at the corner of his bed. She was ashamed of the act she intended to do, but was firm in her resolve to find out the truth. A profound sense of guilt overwhelmed her, but she tried to console herself. So what? After all he is my son. I have carried him in my womb for nine months. No doubt he has grown up, but in my eyes he is still a kid. I washed his butt when he was a child, I gave him baths. When he was down with fever, I changed his underwear. So, why should I feel ashamed? God forgive me, my intentions are not immoral, she tried to salve her conscience. Then, gathering up courage, she slowly removed his blanket and brushed his lungi aside. She placed her quivering hand on his penis beneath the underwear.

It was erect.

The moment she felt its stiffness, she was relieved. All her doubts were cleared.

Mohanaswamy felt the touch and opened his eyes. He was bewildered to see his mother sitting next to him. What's going on? Did my mother just touch my cock? Mohanaswamy was appalled.

'What is this, Amma?' he asked, straightening up his lungi.

Subhadramma broke down. 'What do you know of a mother's plight? The whole town is inquisitive about your manhood. And you are not telling me the truth. What else could I have done?'

Mohanaswamy understood the situation but did not know how to react.

After sobbing for a while, Subhadramma muttered, 'God is great. The fruit of my womb is a boy. Now I don't have to fear anybody or anything.' She caressed his head, planted a kiss on his forehead and said, 'Now you sleep peacefully.' She then headed to the puja room, lit the lamp with wicks dipped in ghee, joined her palms in front of the idol and murmured, 'I know you will not leave me. I believe in you.' She then went to her husband, woke him up and broke the news, 'My son is a man. Let there be no doubts about it.'

Mohanaswamy trembled inwardly and sighed with helplessness. How could he explain to his mother that his cock rose because he was fantasizing about a nude young man in his dream? He couldn't sleep that night. He left for Bengaluru early next morning.

When Mohanaswamy was in pre-university college, his father once went to Ballari to take part in the matrimonial talks of his friend's son. After much negotiation, it was decided that the bride's father should give fifty thousand rupees in cash, two kilograms of silver, forty sovereigns of gold, a Bajaj scooter and a wristwatch to the groom as dowry. Both parties signed the draft paper and Subbaraya signed as a witness. But his hands shook as he signed, imagining his son's bleak future. I will never get such honour in my life because our Mohanaswamy is invalid. He cannot get married. He cannot fetch a dowry. He cannot continue my family line. I will not even attain heaven after death because if he performs my last rites, it would never amount to a son's duties. Because of him, I am not even in a position to hold my head up in society, Subbaraya thought and grew disconcerted. He ceased to have any love or affection for Mohanaswamy. He considered that any money spent on him would be a waste. All his demands irritated him. His wife's adulation for Mohanaswamy annoyed him even more.

The results of Mohanaswamy's entrance exams were out. He had passed with a good rank and got admission in a reputed government engineering college in Bengaluru. When the entire town was celebrating Mohanaswamy's success, his father seemed sick, anxiety writ large on his face. If his son joined an engineering college, the minimum fees would be fifty thousand rupees plus the cost of food, hostel accommodation and travelling between Bengaluru and the town. Should he really spend so much on this boy, who would neither get married nor continue his family name? Wouldn't it be wiser to spend the same money on his daughter's wedding?

Subbaraya indirectly told his son not to join the engineering college but to continue graduation in the town and then take up a clerical job. But Mohanaswamy was determined.

'He is our only son. We must help him go to Bengaluru and study engineering. We can apply for a bank loan. Else, I will sell a few of my gold ornaments,' Subhadramma insisted.

But Subbaraya did not budge. However, when Mohanaswamy remained determined, he said he could go, on the condition that he would manage his expenses on his own.

So finally Mohanaswamy set off for Bengaluru. How long could he stay there without financial support from parents? Subbaraya assumed that his son would throw in the towel and come back sooner than later. But he was wrong. Mohanaswamy did not return. Nor did he ask his father for money. His father too did not dare to ask him how he earned his keep.

Thereafter, whenever Mohanaswamy came home, his father began avoiding him. After he took up a job and started sending some money home every month, his father did not have the courage to touch it. When he bore the entire cost of his sister's wedding, his father sank even more. He started repenting. Why did I do injustice to my own son, who is such a polite, harmless soul? I just went by his sexuality and ignored the other aspects of his personality. Why was I so bothered that he would not fetch dowry from marriage? He is now earning hundredfold more than the dowry money and supports us in every way. He has been touring many countries in the world. When I complained of chest pain, he took me to Bengaluru and got the best treatment done in a big hospital. When his mother had knee pain, he got the knee replacement surgery done for her. So what if he is not married? Subbaraya recalled how the friend's son, who married a Ballari girl after demanding a handsome dowry money, had thrown his parents out of their own house. Neither was he taking good care of his wife. Of course, he has fathered two kids, but then what's the big deal about that?

Many times he thought of confiding in his son and pleading forgiveness. But he could not gather the courage and kept postponing it year after year. Now death was knocking at his door. He tried speaking but his feeble voice failed him. He tried writing a message but his frail, shivering hands did not cooperate. Mohana, my Mohana, please pardon me. As a father, I failed in my duties towards you. I meted out injustice to you. I shouldn't have done that. Please forgive me, my child ... Come fast, I will hold your hands and beg your pardon. Come home ... come home fast...

One evening, after completing the thirteen-day rituals following his father's death, Mohanaswamy went to the priest Gopala Bhatta's house at his mother's behest. 'Poor Brahmin, he seems to be in some problem. He wants to speak to you. Go and meet him,' his mother had insisted. Gopala Bhatta had administered the funeral rites of his father on the banks of the river Tungabhadra in Hampi. His wife had cooked food on all the thirteen days. Though Mohanaswamy did not believe in all those cumbersome rituals, he performed them mundanely, following Gopala Bhatta's instructions. Pinda, specially prepared rice balls, were laid on a banana leaf and offered to crows, with the customary belief that feeding the crows would amount to feeding the departed soul.

But not a single crow came down to eat the pinda. All the people standing there made 'caw, caw' sounds trying to attract the crows flying above, but the birds simply refused to oblige. That in turn indicated that some unfulfilled desire of the dead prevented the soul from attending liberation. Mohanaswamy's mother started sobbing. Someone in the crowd turned to the family members and asked if they knew about any unfulfilled wishes of Subbaraya.

'He desperately wanted to see his son married. He had expressed it to me many times. That's why he is refusing to have his food today...' Mohanaswamy's mother said, as her eyes welled up.

Mohanaswamy stood unmoved. His sister Janaki, who was consoling her crying baby on her lap, told him gruffly, 'Go, Mohana, go and pray. Why are you inviting flak from everyone?'

But Mohanaswamy did not budge.

'I know he will not agree. When his father was alive he did not agree to get married. Even now he is not willing to commit himself. I know he will not,' his mother cried.

The crowd insisted that he must go and pray. Mohanaswamy was furious. Finally, it was Gopala Bhatta who came out with an amicable solution. 'Mohana Rao, do one thing. Go and stand near the pillar and pray whatever you feel is right. There is no need to say it publicly.'

Backed into a corner, Mohanaswamy reluctantly rose and walked towards the pillar where the pinda was placed. What would he pray for? Who knew what was there on father's mind before his death? The image of his father on his death bed, holding his hands and weeping, came before his eyes.

Standing in front of the pillar, Mohanaswamy joined his palms together and prayed in his mind. 'Appa, I don't know what your problem is. If you want to have food, you may please come down and have it. If you don't want, just leave it. I can't get married for the sake of your one-time meal. I don't want to ruin the life of a woman by marrying her. I don't want to live a life that is not mine. Please don't expect that from me. You don't have the right to do so,' he said impassively.

Then the miracle happened. A crow swooped down from somewhere, nibbled at the rice and darted back to the sky. 'You performed a miracle, Mohana Rao,' said Gopala Bhatta.

'I knew it, that was indeed my husband's deepest desire...' Subhadramma shed tears of joy.

'In that case, we should start looking out for a bride for Mohana,' said some relatives jokingly, to which the entire crowd cheered.

During the rituals that followed, it was the son of the deceased who had to lift the plantain leaves after the Brahmins had eaten on them. If he was married, he could take his wife's help in the cleaning work. Mohanaswamy found it too cumbersome. He reluctantly hitched up his dhoti and bent down to lift the leaves. He wasn't used to such chores ever since he joined college. Piling on the agony was the extremely humid climate. Seeing

Mohanaswamy sweating it out on his own, someone among the relatives commented, 'Had he got married he wouldn't have faced this problem.'

Mohanaswamy was at the end of his tether. A few drops of tears slid down his cheeks. Feeling miserable, he felt like running back to Bengaluru. Gopala Bhatta understood his plight. 'My son, this is an age-old tradition which can be amended. You can take the help of some womenfolk in the cleaning work, no problem,' said the priest. Then Mohanaswamy's sister Janaki came to his rescue.

Since Gopala Bhatta had saved him a few times on such occasions, Mohanaswamy had developed some respect for him. So when his mother told him that the priest wanted to see him, he went off to visit him without thinking twice.

~

It was dusk when Mohanaswamy reached Gopala Bhatta's town. The Tungabhadra river was flowing quietly at a distance. On its stretched banks was the lone mud house of the priest. Around it, huge boulders stood supporting one another. Someone had drawn a picture of Hanuman on one of the boulders. It was spattered with vermilion and turmeric. A crow perched on the boulder and cawed loudly. Gopala Bhatta was sitting in the front yard, fanning himself with a handmade fan and reading a newspaper. Abutting the front yard was a cowshed where two cows were chewing fodder. A huge rangoli was drawn in front of the house and it was surrounded by a few flower pots.

'Please come, please come,' Gopala Bhatta received Mohanaswamy affectionately. He spread a mat on the stone platform and asked him to sit on it. 'Oye…' he called out and his daughter peeped from inside. 'Amma has gone to the temple for bhajan,' she said, glancing at Mohanaswamy. A beautiful face, Mohanaswamy said to himself. 'Get a glass of coffee,' her father told her. She disappeared inside.

'Did you find any difficulty in locating our house? It is quite far from the town,' the priest opened the conversation.

'No … not at all. Everyone in town knows your address. They guided me,' said Mohanaswamy.

'Earlier our house was on the chariot street. It was so convenient. We were staying there since our father's time. But what to do? The government vacated us from there,' the priest rued.

His daughter, wearing a cotton sari, came back with a glass of coffee, kept it in front of him and went back. A diminutive lady, must be in her early thirties. The coffee smelled and tasted good, made of fresh cow-milk. 'My mother told me that you wanted to speak to me, what's the matter?' Mohanaswamy asked the priest, sipping the hot coffee.

Gopala Bhatta swallowed nervously before beginning, 'The girl who came with the coffee is my daughter, Anjali. She is thirty-two, a very intelligent girl. She is the one who drew that big beautiful rangoli in the front yard. She has watered and raised all these plants that you see around. She is a very good cook too. Unfortunately her husband died four years ago. He committed suicide. It seems he had misappropriated funds at the mines department. Fearing that the government authorities might take action and put him in jail, he jumped onto the railway tracks and came under the Hampi Express.'

Mohanaswamy did not understand why Gopala Bhatta was telling him all this. The priest continued, 'My daughter's world fell apart after her husband's death. Her in-laws were not ready to keep her. I had borrowed a lot of money to marry her off. The loan amount is still pending, but already she is back at home. I feel sad every time I pay the monthly instalment,' he said, wiping his tears with the hem of his dhoti.

Mohanaswamy remained silent. Maybe he will ask for some financial help, he thought. 'Tell me, how can I help you?'

'You are a big man ... a learned man ... You understand

everything. You must somehow hold my daughter's hand and help her...'

'Sorry, I don't quite understand.'

'If you marry her, you will get some support and we will also be relieved of our burden,' the priest said explicitly.

Mohanaswamy was mum for a while. 'I am sorry, Gopala Bhatta. I have no intentions of getting married and settling down with a wife. Otherwise, why would I remain unmarried even after forty?' he said without missing a beat.

'Not like that, Mohana Rao, I am elder to you. Please don't misunderstand me. You will need someone to look after you in old age. A man should not live alone. Life after forty is very tough. It is always advisable to have a companion who can take care of you...' the priest said, trying to twist his arm into marrying his daughter.

Mohanaswamy was irritated. 'In what words shall I tell you that I don't want to get married? Why are you forcing me?' he said, and got up to go.

But Gopala Bhatta did not stop. He said hesitatingly, 'After marriage, if you don't want to sleep with her, it's okay. I will not force you. I will clearly tell my daughter not to expect it. But she will be cooking, cleaning and doing other chores for you. She will take good care of you. All in all, she will live with you as a friend, is that fine? She will get a new life and you too can avoid nagging questions from people for not getting married.'

Mohanaswamy was flummoxed by this implausible offer. At the same time, the fact that the Brahmin had found out about his sexuality riled him up. He guessed that his mother must have had a role in this scheme of things. Even then, deciding not to lose his temper, he said tactfully, 'I can get domestic help in the city very easily. I don't need a wife just for that. I can't marry someone with whom I can't share my bed. I don't have faith in such a marriage. I can't put on an act in front of the world.'

'Then that is your wish. If you feel I have crossed my limits, please forgive me,' the priest said, his hands folded. He followed Mohanaswamy to the gate to see him off. When they reached the gate, Mohanaswamy saw Bhatta's wife at a distance. He knew her well as she had accompanied her husband during his father's rituals. But who was that young man with her? He squinted to see through the dim streetlight. When they approached the gate, Mohanaswamy was startled to realize who that handsome young man was.

It was Derrick.

The same twenty-five-year-old Derrick with that pencil moustache, whose soft skin, warm breath and tender body had held Mohanaswamy in thrall. But he looked so different in this avatar – donning a white dhoti and a light blue shirt, vibhuti and vermillion on his forehead.

For Derrick too, it was a bolt from the blue. His face fell at the sight of Mohanaswamy. Gopala Bhatta introduced him. 'He is my son, Ramesh. He was studying engineering, but dropped out in the third year as he found it hard. Since then he has not found himself a job. I have heard that you work for a big company. Can you help him get some job and settle down?' the priest pleaded.

Mohanaswamy was in a dither, not knowing how to react. Regaining his composure, he asked Ramesh, 'What do you do in Bengaluru?'

The boy did not reply.

'Speak up, Ramesh. Our Mohanaswamy is a big man. He will help you out. It is high time you stopped loafing around and took up some responsibility in life,' his father said with asperity.

Ramesh opened his mouth. 'I am doing some odd jobs ... But I am not able to get full-time employment,' he babbled, bowing his head in shame.

His reply brought a cheer to Mohanaswamy's face. 'Then you do one thing. You keep coming to my house in Bengaluru every now and then. I'm available in the evenings. We can discuss the matter in detail. Something or the other will work out. Let me see how I can help you,' he said.

'If you do that I will be grateful to you Mohana Rao. You did not agree to hold my daughter's hand. Never mind. But kindly help my son,' Gopala Bhatta said in joy.

Then turning to his son he asked him, 'You will go to his house, won't you?'

Ramesh nodded with a bashful grin.

BED BUG

My childhood friend Shankar Gowda used to come to school from a village that was about two kilometres away from my hometown. He was the youngest son of the Gowda, the head of the village, and their family had land, money and power. Shankar Gowda was tall, fair and well-built. He could have easily been the prince of any girl's dreams. But god wasn't so kind to him.

His speech, voice, the way he walked and his tastes were all effeminate. Shankar Gowda was the butt of many jokes at school. It was all too common for boys to taunt him, imitating his soft, delicate way of speaking and his girlish gait.

It was not just his classmates – even the teachers

made fun of him. Once during a biology lesson, the teacher was telling the class that sometimes, due to chromosomal mismatch, a child is born neither girl nor boy. As he said this, his eyes wandered across to Shankar Gowda and he broke into a nasty smile. The entire class shouted 'Shankara Gowda' and burst into laughter.

But Shankar Gowda wasn't cowed by such remarks. In fact, he would join in with the laughter. Indeed, his behaviour quite warranted their remarks. He would sing P. Susheela's '*Hoovu Cheluvella Tandenditu*' in a sweet, girlish voice. He would fill the end pages of his notebooks with rangoli designs. When he spotted designer saris displayed in garment shops, he would admire the patterns, transfixed. He had no interest in sports like kabaddi and volleyball, instead, he delighted in playing tennikoit with the girls. Wiggling his body, he entertained us with his imitations of prostitutes in his village and solicited young men, calling out, 'Brother, come to me in the night, brother!' This would send everyone into fits of laughter. He would repeat this performance any number of times for our amusement.

Shankar Gowda always sat next to me in class. He wasn't very good with his lessons and needed my help. He would copy my notes and in return, he would bring me gooseberries, wood apples, jamun fruit and sweet tamarind pods from his village. Sometimes he gave me the rangoli designs that he drew in his notebooks. He was so sweet-natured, I had no qualms being friends with him.

But to his ostentatious family, his effeminate behaviour was a bitter pill to swallow. His two brothers, his father, mother and everyone else in his family implored him to change. How could he change something that was natural to him?

Once, he did not come to school for three days. The boys in his village said that he was ill. On the fourth day, he arrived looking very pale. After school, when I asked him what had happened, he took me behind the school building. There, where no one else could see, he removed his shirt and lowered his pants. There were deep welts and black bruises all over his body. I was horrified. Shankar told me that his father and brothers had locked him in a room and whipped him to beat his girlish ways out of him. Afterwards, they told everyone that Shankar Gowda was ill. They did not even bother taking him to a doctor. Only his mother smeared coconut oil over his wounds.

Something shifted in Shankar after this incident and he became more subdued. The school annual day was drawing near, and our teacher decided to make us enact 'Draupadi Vastrapaharan'. But which girl would be willing to perform the role of Draupadi being disrobed in court? The boys suggested that Shankar Gowda be given the role – and the teacher agreed.

But Shankar baulked at the idea. 'My father will kill me! I will not play a female character.' The teacher tried to persuade him but in vain. Another boy was chosen for the part. On the annual day, Shankar Gowda walked into the green room as his classmates were dressing up for the play. He went over to the boy in Draupadi's costume and caressed the soft silk sari, felt the blouse and ornaments.

After completing my PUC, I moved to another city to study engineering. I began to lose touch with my childhood friends. I heard that Shankar Gowda failed in PUC once, appeared again, passed, and joined a local college to pursue his BA.

On my rare visits to my hometown, Shankar would invariably learn of my presence and try to meet me. But I avoided him. He would continue to bring gooseberries, guavas and tamarind pods for me. As I no longer relished his attention, I gave these things away to others. Once, just as I was leaving to return to college, he came to the bus stand and handed me a parcel. When the bus drove out of town, I opened the package. Inside, I found expensive body lotion, powder, shampoo and bottles of aromatic oils, and a note saying, 'I want my friend to look beautiful'. Worried that someone might see it, I hid the pack until the bus reached Gandi Narasimhaswamy hill. I threw it down into the valley, heaving a huge sigh of relief.

After I completed my engineering, I found myself a job in a reputed software company in Bengaluru. With time, my bitterness towards Shankar Gowda mellowed and I started to develop a soft corner for him again. He continued to look me up whenever I visited my hometown. It was heart-wrenching to watch him drift into futility and nothingness, unable to complete his BA and damned constantly by his family.

Once, when he came to see me, I asked him, 'How is your father now?'

'Now he can't have it his way,' Shankar replied with a guffaw. 'He came to scold me, but I lashed back and hit him black and blue with a whip. He was in the hospital for fifteen days. Now that bolimaga, son of a shaved widow, never dares to cross my path.'

I suggested that he find himself a job.

'Who will give me a job?' he giggled.

He told me that he had gone for an interview for a peon's post in a local office. There were three men on the interview board. They asked him, 'What are you good at?' Shankar Gowda replied honestly, 'I can sing and dance well.'

'Well then, show us how good you are,' they said.

He danced in front of them in the interview room, singing, '*Ghil Ghil Ghil Ghilakku, Kalu Gejje Jhalakku…*' His show evoked peals of laughter from them.

'Wonderful!' they exclaimed and applauded as he finished. They promised him a job but he never heard from them again. After this, he lost interest in taking up a job.

Another time, he took me to visit a Hanuman temple on the outskirts of my hometown. A mutual friend Kumarswamy, Kommi as we called him, ran a garment shop which would fall on the way.

I wanted to meet him and so we went by his shop. 'Lo … Kommee…' Shankar Gowda hollered from a distance. Kommi, busy showing garments to his customers, raised his hand to shoo him away contemptuously as one would do to a beggar. Unfazed, Shankar Gowda shouted again, 'I know you are a big man. I am not asking you to talk to me. But look who has come!' Upon hearing his words, Kommi turned and catching sight of me, he stopped his work.

'When did you come, maaraya?' he exclaimed. 'Come, come inside.' He took my hand, led me inside the shop and offered me a cool drink. Shankar Gowda followed us. Still holding my hand, Kommi chatted with me for fifteen minutes, but he never bothered to look at Shankar Gowda, let alone talk to him.

Just as we were leaving, Shankar Gowda asked, 'By the way, Kommanna, how's Chandravva doing?'

That sent Kommi into a rage. 'Son of a slut!' He raised his hand in anger to strike Shankar, but he dodged the blow and dashed out of the shop, laughing hysterically.

I didn't understand what was happening and asked Kommi, 'Who is Chandravva?'

'That swine blabbers nonsense, just leave it! Loose-tongued son of a whore,' Kommi growled.

I joined Shankar Gowda at the corner of the street. 'She is his keep – for the past two years,' he explained. 'She stays behind the Durgamma temple. He's even got her a gold necklace!' he added naughtily.

There was no one in the Hanuman temple when we reached there. It was cool and quiet. A bird was singing sweetly in a crape jasmine tree that had formed a canopy over the temple entrance. The fragrance filled the air. We prostrated before the idol, cupped our palms over the flame of an oil-lamp placed in a corner and raised them to our eyes. Shankar Gowda paused and applied a dab of kumkum on his forehead. He applied some kumkum on my forehead too, carefully dusting off the specks.

After we had sat in silence for a while, I said, 'Gowda, you must get married.'

He laughed so hard that tears filled his eyes. Then, suddenly serious, he pleaded, 'Please, you also don't start making fun of me.'

I apologized and we walked home in silence.

That night, after dinner, I was sitting on the katte when Kommi came over. 'You are a Bengaluru man,' he said. 'You don't understand what goes on here. Just listen to me. I'm telling you this for your own good.' Saying so, he proceeded to tell me that I should stop roaming around with Shankar Gowda.

'Why do you say so, maaraya? After all he was our classmate.'

'Don't ask me questions so innocently as though you are asking about a math problem to some teacher in school!' Kommi fumed. 'Just try to understand. You are an intelligent boy. There was no one in our town to score marks like you, and there will be no one in the future either. You are the pride of our town. You have a good job in Bengaluru. I'm telling you this not just as a friend, but as an elder brother. Just do as I am telling you. If people in the town speak ill of you, I can't stand it. Stop associating yourself with that son of a bitch.'

Five years passed. My parents moved to Bengaluru to stay with me, and the next time I visited the town was on the occasion of a distant relative's wedding. I was determined to meet Shankar Gowda.

But shocking news awaited me when I reached the wedding hall. Shankar Gowda had committed suicide by hanging himself.

What made Shankar Gowda, who had the guts to lash out his own father with a whip, hang himself?

None of those present at the wedding could give me a convincing answer.

That evening, I headed to his village. It was dark by the time I reached his house. His mother was sitting in the courtyard, sorting and picking menthyasoppu. His father was reclining on a cot, smoking a beedi.

'Who is it?' His mother squinted to catch a better glimpse of me in the dark. 'Whom do you want to see?' His father sat up.

I introduced myself. 'I studied with Shankar Gowda. I live in Bengaluru. I came to the town for a wedding and heard that he passed away.'

His mother wiped her eyes with the hem of her sari.

'Please pardon me,' I continued. 'My intention is not to hurt you. The news of his death pains me. I just want to know why Shankar Gowda suddenly ended his life.'

His mother began to weep in earnest and she went inside. I looked at his father, who was still smoking his beedi.

He took a deep puff, blew the smoke out and crushed the butt on the floor. 'How can we say why the dead choose death? He's dead, that's it. Maybe he was fed up of life, so he went. Maybe he wanted to make us suffer, so he went,' he said acidly.

'No, no, I'm sure that's not the case ... but you would have known the reasons behind his actions...'

'We don't know anything, we don't know,' he said, raising his voice sternly. Shankar Gowda's brothers and their wives came out. 'And how does it matter to you anyway?' he continued, shrilly. 'Who are you, his husband or paramour? We have had a bellyful of our woes and you come in here like a bear. Well, if you still want to know why he died, you too go hang yourself, and then you can catch up with him and find out. Go, get lost!' he pointed to the gate, his hands quivering in rage.

Without saying another word, I left. After walking a few minutes, I turned around. Shankar's mother was standing in the backyard and looking at me. She wants to tell me something, I thought, and started walking towards her. But she turned away at once and went inside. I waited for a long time, hoping she would change her mind. But she did not come back.

On the way home, I stopped by to visit Kommi. He was married and had a two-year-old son. He introduced his wife to me, a BCom graduate from

Hagaribommanahalli village. Kommi spoke fondly of his son's mischievous pranks.

After some time, I asked him, 'Why did Shankar Gowda commit suicide?'

Kommi did not reply. He turned to his son. 'Sweetie,' he pushed his son towards the kitchen, 'go to your mother.' Kommi turned back to me. 'When will you go back to Bengaluru?'

'Tomorrow.'

'Then why do you want to dig into all this? Just leave peacefully.' But I couldn't let it go. I sat there, quietly, looking at Kommi. Finally, his restraint cracked. 'Well, come let's go out.'

He took me to an eatery in the outskirts. 'I don't drink,' I said.

'I know, but I must. Otherwise things like this cannot be said,' he snapped. He ordered a drink and a snack. Then he began, 'Brother, this town is no longer what it used to be. But you are the same, like you used to be as a small boy. You are a good human being. Unlike us, you did not adopt any vices. But the town is not like you.' He went on in this fashion for a while, spouting amateur philosophy.

Eventually I ran out of patience. I grabbed his glass and pulled it towards me. 'Tell me. How did he die?'

By now Kommi was slightly drunk. He looked

straight into my eyes and said, 'He did not die. They killed him.'

'Who?'

'His father and brothers. They killed him and then hanged him.' He snatched his glass back and downed what was left in one swig.

I was shocked to the point of tears. 'He was the son of the house, born and raised there. How could they kill him?'

Kommi poured himself another drink. He took a few swigs before replying. 'You know a bed bug, right? It slips into the mattress and bites you all through the night, disturbing your sleep. That son of a bitch was like a bed bug. Just because a bed bug is born in the house people live and grows up there, will they shower love on it? No. If they spot it, they will squish it and wash their hands clean. This is exactly what his father and brothers did to him. One day, when he was asleep, they smothered him with a pillow. Then they used his blanket to hang his body, and created a big scene next morning, beating their breasts.'

'Who told you all this?'

'The entire town knows it, not just me. Those three men struggled to keep it under wraps. But how could Shankar's mother conceal her grief? She told some people and cried her heart out. Those who heard her story consoled her, and in turn told others.'

I sighed. 'He always minded his own business. What made them kill him? It's a heinous crime!'

'Not so fast, not so fast. I haven't finished yet. If he'd minded his own business, nobody would have done this to him.'

'What was his sin that he deserved death?' I fumed.

'He ran away to Mumbai. Stayed there for six months. He got his dick chopped off and came back wearing a sari and blouse.'

I was dumbstruck.

Kommi continued, slurring slightly now, 'It was Ugadi, the chariot festival day. The shepherd boys were beating drums. The Nandi Kolu performer was dancing. Suddenly a person storms in, dancing away to the drummers' beat. Looked like a film heroine. We all wondered who this lady was and where she came from. Youths began shaking and gyrating with her, matching her vigour. Nobody realized it was Shankar. When the chariot drove into the yard of Basavanna temple, my wife and I bowed to the god in worship, Shankar came near us. "Kommanna, how's Chandravva?" he cackled and went away. That is when I realized who it was. I was newly married. All hell broke loose as my wife stiffened and began to nag me about who Chandravva was. I had a hard time pacifying her.'

'From the next day onwards, he began his antics. He came straight to my shop. "I want five bras and five panties" he would say coquettishly. I told him to get out. But he had become bold and brazen. "I will buy whatever I want. What's your problem?" he retorted, and left only after purchasing all the stuff he wanted. The news began to spread. People hounded his father and brothers with all sorts of questions.' Kommi paused, before going on. 'Tell me, what do you expect them to do when their boy turns into a woman, wrapping himself up in a sari? They tried throwing him out of the house. "I also have a share in the property in this house," Shankar would assert, sticking to his guns. "Share in the property is only for the sons, not for daughters," his brothers replied. I don't know who in Mumbai had helped him get his courage so high, but he simply refused to leave the house. He ate there, bathed there and slept there.

'But his antics did not stop at that. He began luring the men in the town into his trap, one by one. His looks were exactly like a woman. He was stunning, believe me, women in our town were no match for him. His waist, his thighs, buttocks and breasts – he had got them all done. Men started going to him, one by one. He ran it like a business. Women at home began showering curses on him. His family members hung their heads in shame, unable to face the villagers. Not just that, the senior Gowda, who had never tasted defeat in a panchayat election before, lost that year.

'For how long could they put up with such indignity? Their family had lived respectably in the village for years. They grew weary and lost their patience.' Kommi was drunk to the point that he would disclose anything. 'Finally his father and brothers bumped him off. Now everyone is at peace in the village.'

'Instead of killing him, they could have given him his share in the property!' I countered. 'If they'd given him some money, he could have bought himself a house and lived elsewhere peacefully.'

'Arre arre arre … here you go wrong again. He had no dearth of money. He ran a roaring business. When he died, I heard that he had one and a half lakh rupees in his account. He had made his mother the nominee. Will anybody let go of money? Both the sons took their mother to the bank and withdrew the entire amount. Money wasn't the actual problem. The problem was his pig-headedness – he insisted on staying in the house, claiming his rights. Tell me, what kind of madness was that?' Kommi roared with laughter.

I felt my stomach churning.

'See brother, this isn't something you should feel sad about. He was sleeping around with just about any man. I'm sure, one day or the other, he would have got AIDS. He would have suffered and died but not before spreading the disease to the entire town. In fact, his father and brothers only did a favour by killing him before that happened.'

I didn't want to hear any more. I paid the bill and hauled Kommi out of the eatery.

Still drunk, Kommi raved about Shankar Gowda's acquired womanhood. 'Whatever you say, that whore was such a spotless beauty, the kind one should only touch with clean hands. The way she wore a sari! The way she wore a matching blouse, the chain around her neck, bangles on her wrists, perfume, powder! Wow!' I listened to his words in disgust until we finally reached his house. 'Good night,' he said, shaking my hand drunkenly.

'Kommi,' I said. 'I want to ask you something. Will you tell me the truth?'

'Ask, my lord, ask whatever you want. I will tell the truth, and nothing but the truth,' he said, as if testifying in court, and began laughing at his own foolery.

'Did you too enjoy Shankar Gowda?'

Kommi's laughter came to an abrupt halt and he dropped my hand. He walked to his door, then turned back. 'If someone sleeps next to me, touching, pawing and canoodling, how I am supposed to control myself? I am a man, I have a dick. What applies to other men in the town – it is only fair that it applies to me as well.'

He strode briskly into the house and slammed the door shut.

THE UNPALATABLE OFFERING

Mohanaswamy lost his bearings completely when he saw the building. It looked as though it had jetted out from under the earth, splitting the surface wide apart. It was an eight-storey apartment complex, still under construction. Hundreds of people were busy at work. The place was filled with the bustle of labourers, supervisors and machines. Cranes, taller than the building, were lifting and placing loads from one place to another. How did such mammoth machines come strolling here? Mohanaswamy pondered. There was dust everywhere. Sand, cement, iron rods and bricks lay scattered. A narrow path through that clutter led to a signboard which read, 'Way to the apartment office'. Strangely, that board was clean and free of dust.

I shouldn't have come here, Mohanaswamy thought. In fact, until an hour back, he had no plans of going there. Why would the idea of purchasing a house come to Mohanaswamy when he was all set to leave for a foreign country the next evening for four years? Last evening, he had gone to his friend Gururaja's house for a quick farewell. He had hoped that his wife would offer him some home-cooked food he had been craving for long. Gururaja would often ask him to stay back for lunch or dinner. 'No Guru, I don't want anything. Why do you take the trouble? I just had my food', Mohanaswamy would say, but Gururaja wouldn't listen. 'So what? Have some more,' he would urge him affectionately. This gesture would melt Mohanaswamy's heart and fearing that his voice may choke with tears, he would just nod his head.

At first he used to pity himself for his desperate hankering for food at Gururaja's house. He would say a strict no and then go to a nearby Darshini, the fast-food chain, for dinner. But of late, if someone offered him home-made food, he ate it without leaving a tiny bit on his plate. Sometimes, he even asked for a second serving without hesitation.

Gururaja understood his friend's pain and loneliness all too well. So, without raking up his woes, he would, in his authority as a friend, often ask him to eat at his place. They had been close friends for the last fifteen years, right from their college days. Mohanaswamy took comfort in the fact that he was not physically drawn to this friend. It was a matter of great relief that though he shared a bed with Gururaja on several occasions, he never felt the urge to touch him. In the past, many friendships had gone sour in a moment that Mohanaswamy then regretted for months. His efforts to mend these broken bonds would be in vain. He was constantly afraid that he would lose all his friends one day and would be shrouded in loneliness. 'How will I live without friends? Hey Krishna, save my friendship with Gururaja. May my evil eye not befall him,' he often prayed.

Some young boys had come to Gururaja's house that evening. Clad in dhotis and bright shalyas and wearing naama – religious identification marks – prominently on their bodies, the boys were evidently busy. Gururaja's mother explained the occasion, 'Today is Subraya's Shrashti. I have invited five bachelor boys to hand them the offering of sacred thread and a towel. I have been afflicted with Naga Dosha since birth. It seems my grandfather had killed a pair of cobras while building a house. That curse came upon me. I remained unmarried for many years. Finally, somebody advised me to observe Subraya's Shrashti, and I did. It paid off. I got a proposal, got married and had children. Since then I have been observing this rite every year without fail.'

Gururaja's wife served hot dosas to Mohanaswamy. 'We won't get to see him for the next four years. He is going abroad. Serve him more dosas,' Gururaja told her, extending warm hospitality to his friend. Gururaja's little son Aniketa was sitting on Mohanaswamy's lap, pulling off his spectacles and knocking off the pen, paper chits and mobile phone from his pocket. Mohanaswamy fondly took the child's tiny hands in his hand and brushed them against his cheeks, enjoying the divine touch. 'Anee, don't trouble Uncle,' Gururaja chided, but the child continued playing, with intermittent peals of laughter. Every now and then, he pestered Mohanaswamy for a piece of dosa. But Mohanaswamy did not dare to place even a morsel from his plate into the boy's mouth. 'Go ask your mother. You are a good boy, aren't you?' he consoled the child.

Suddenly a thought flashed through Gururaja's mind. 'Mohana, you said you won't be coming back for the next four or five years. Why don't you buy yourself an apartment before you leave? I'm sure money won't be a problem. You can even apply for a loan if required. By the time you are back, the loan amount would have shrunk considerably. And you would have your own house to live in!' he said.

Mohanaswamy panicked at the idea. He had never thought of buying a house. All his friends had already bought houses and held house-warming ceremonies, serving sumptuous meals to guests. Mohanaswamy had attended all these ceremonies, giving gifts and savouring food to his heart's content.

He remembered Gururaja narrating the difficulties of building a house. He used to take Mohanaswamy along with him for some work or the other like giving documents to contractors, buying lamps from Avenue Road, meeting a lawyer at his office on St Marks Road and so on. But Mohanaswamy never felt the urge to have his own house. It did not seem relevant to him. When his parents were alive, they had raised the matter a couple of times, but after their death, there was no one to bring it up again.

'What will I do with a house? It is meant for family men like you,' he said, laughing sheepishly.

'A bachelor or a family man, shelling out large sums of money for house rent in this damned city is nothing but foolishness. If you have a roof over your head, it gives you so much peace of mind. Don't go for an independent house. A flat in an apartment complex will serve your needs better. Security and maintenance won't be a headache. A good complex is coming up about four kilometres away from here and I have heard many people in my office booking flats there. You should book one for yourself before going abroad. You can either come back for registration, or I will get it done for you,' Gururaja urged him.

Mohanaswamy considered the proposal for a while. If he owned a house he wouldn't have to put up with pesky landlords, he thought. Of course, landlords had never really troubled him so far. He left for office in the morning only to return in the evening. Moreover, he had a predilection for keeping the house spotlessly clean. He used minimum water, created no nuisance and paid rent promptly every month, even agreeing to the ten per cent annual increment. Which landlord wouldn't like to have such a tenant? Even then, wasn't it better to have one's own house?

Right then Gururaja's mother interrupted his thoughts. 'Mohana, you have come at the right time. We had invited five brahmachari boys for the puja, but only four turned up. You be the fifth one and accept the tambula,' she said.

He was quite embarrassed. 'Aunty, I am already thirty-five. How can you count me as a brahmachari?' he asked with bashful smile.

'So what, you aren't married yet, right? That makes you a brahmachari. Now don't delay my puja. Come, accept the offering of sacred thread and towel,' she instructed.

He looked at Gururaja. 'Go and take it, nothing will happen,' Gururaja said.

Mohanaswamy sat with those four young boys and received the tambula. The boys chuckled, looking at the uncle sitting next to them, almost their fathers' age. Mohanaswamy was amused too and laughed along with them. After accepting the offerings, the boys bent low in obeisance to Gururaja's mother. She blessed them saying, 'Study well and pass with good marks.' But when Mohanaswamy bowed, she pronounced, 'Get married soon.'

The mention of marriage didn't scare Mohanaswamy these days. Instead, a hope sprang up in his heart. How beautiful life would be if this mother's blessings brought about a miraculous change in me, kindling a desire for females, he thought. Then I too could get married and settle down! He dreamt on, but soon realized the futility of his musings. 'May your wish come true, Aunty. Then I will buy you whatever you demand,' said Mohanaswamy.

'You just say yes, and I will put a garland of brides around your neck!' she said with a laugh and went inside.

'Oye, will you get married?' Gururaja asked, teasing his friend.

'You keep quiet my friend, don't make fun of me,' Mohanaswamy said in his old usual style.

When Mohanaswamy was preparing to leave, Gururaja insisted again that he should immediately go to the apartment complex and look for a flat. Knowing that his dear friend wouldn't relent, Mohanaswamy decided to give it a go. 'You please come with me,' he requested Gururaja, but he was busy. 'My wife wants me to go with her to some place, Mohana. You go and see the house. Just make sure that water, electricity, generator, lift and all other amenities are in place. I will give you some more tips tonight,' he said.

Mohanaswamy did not feel all that bad. About seven-eight years ago, he wouldn't go anywhere without the company of his friends. Be it for going to a shop to buy a handkerchief or to see a movie or to a restaurant for coffee, he would need some company. He would forget the whole world, prattling, laughing and arguing with them. But as time passed, all his friends got married and were no longer easily available. Whenever he phoned them, they would speak for a while and hang up, saying 'I am a little busy, will call you later'. In a couple of years, they all had children. Then they were not even available on phone.

So Mohanaswamy started getting used to being alone and feeling lonely. Initially he would stay home, doing nothing. But for how long could he live like that? Left with no option, he began going out alone, for movies, to buy clothes and even to tourist spots. At first, he felt frightened to roam around all by himself. When he sat in an ice-cream parlour polishing off a big Gudbud alone, he felt uneasy and the ice-cream tasted bitter. He felt like everyone in the parlour was staring at him. But slowly he got used to all this. He reminded himself that he was completely free now – he could go home at any hour, he could wake up late and he could go anywhere – there was no one to question him. Yet sometimes his loneliness would bring him a lot of misery.

One day in office, he suddenly developed a severe stomach ache. He doubled up with pain. He had never had it so bad before. He couldn't even walk. His colleagues were about to call in a doctor when the pain subsided. Full of fear and anxiety, he went to a hospital the next day.

Mohanaswamy loved hospitals. Doctors and nurses speak to you with so much concern! You become their centre of attention. 'Does it pain?' nurses ask you with so much care! Doctors too listen to you with rapt attention.

After examining Mohanaswamy, the doctor asked him to get an endoscopy done. And so he bravely went to the hospital again the next day, all alone. His stomach had been completely empty from the previous night. He didn't have a clue about endoscopy. He had imagined that it must be something akin to a blood test or a BP check-up. But it was not that simple. The test required him to lie down on the bed with his hands and legs strapped up. A long rubber pipe would be slipped into his stomach through his mouth. A camera affixed to the end of the pipe would scan the inside of his abdomen and display the images on the screen.

The nurse had to struggle a lot to insert the pipe into Mohanaswamy's stomach. Whenever the pipe slid past his throat, he panicked, writhing in acute agony. He wanted to take the pipe out and throw it away, but he couldn't do so as his hands and legs were tied. He squirmed in pain and the nurse had to take out the pipe. Though he was on an empty stomach, he threw up some water and that caused further pain.

'You must relax. Otherwise we won't be able to do the test,' the nurse told him repeatedly. But no matter how hard he tried to stay composed, the moment the pipe went inside his throat, he felt like he was at death's door and he panicked. It took over forty-five minutes for the test to get over. Finally, after the test was over, his limbs were quivering. 'Sir, please relax for a while. Why did you come alone? You should have brought someone along,' the nurse said wearily.

When he came out and sat down on a chair to relax, he was overwhelmed with sorrow. I should have brought a friend along, he said to himself. But who would have come with him, taking leave from office? He felt dejected. The only solace was that the doctors who went over his medical reports told him, 'You are fine. You don't have any serious problem. The stomach ache was due to gas trouble, that's all.'

So they sent him away. Mohanaswamy knew that if his health ever took a bad turn, he would be done for and would die alone. Such was his plight that even if he was down with a slight fever, there was no one to boil some gruel for him. No one to remind him to take his medicines in time. And no one to take him to a doctor. So it was imperative that he did not fall sick. Mohanaswamy therefore became more careful and conscious about his health.

But today, the task at hand was simple – just seeing a house. It wasn't mandatory to bring someone along. At the apartment office, he had to wait for over forty-five minutes for his turn. Two families were deliberating over the details of the flats they were planning to buy. A couple were fighting over the design of windows – the husband wanted a French window, but the wife brushed it aside arguing that it lets too much light in. In the other family, it was the wife's parents who were dominating the discussion, raising too many queries. Mohanaswamy guessed that the wife's parents must have given some money to buy the house. The father-in-law insisted on a toilet with an Indian commode while the mother-in-law was arguing that the house would be incomplete without a puja room. The husband was negotiating over the per square feet rate. The couple's children were bored by all this and were about to sneak out to the construction site. The moment the mother realized this, she ran behind them. 'Be careful! Iron rods and nails will prick you!' she screamed, dragging them back in. They started crying. 'Look, Pandu, don't cry. I will tell this uncle to keep a separate room for you in the new house, okay? We will put up all the cartoon posters on the wall,' she told the child, trying to pacify him.

It took over forty-five minutes for both the families to get done with their questions, negotiations and suggestions for changes. The manager, who looked worn out, now came to Mohanaswamy. Though he was visibly exhausted, he beamed a charming smile at Mohanaswamy. 'My name is Rajesh. Sorry, I kept you waiting for long. What type of flat are you looking for, sir? What are your requirements?' he asked.

Mohanaswamy had not come prepared for this question. He had simply come to look at a flat. 'I need a small one,' he replied.

'The smallest we have is a 2 BHK. But sir, when you have set out to buy, why settle for less? Go for a three bedroom house. Once your children grow up, you will need more room,' he suggested.

'I don't really need such a big house. Show me the

smallest you have,' Mohanaswamy repeated with a shrivelled smile.

'Do you care for vastu, sir?'

'No, none of that. Just show me a flat – a small and nice one.'

'Oh, finally someone who doesn't insist on vastu! These days it is easy to build a palace sir, but not so easy to build even a small toilet without considering vastu,' he said with a laugh and asked Mohanaswamy to follow him. Though the apartment complex was still under-construction, a fully-furnished model flat was ready for display.

The door opened to a huge hall. Mohanaswamy was taken aback by its size and hesitated to step inside. He held on to a beam tightly and stood outside the entrance. He came to his senses only when Rajesh alerted him, 'Come inside, sir, no need to remove your shoes.' Mohanaswamy went inside. A big LCD TV was placed in a corner. Surrounding it was a big sofa set. A six-seater dining table stood in another corner. A spacious kitchen and a store room abutted the dining area. There was a separate space to keep the washing machine and refrigerator. The walls were lined with cabinets to arrange utensils and other household items. There were two bedrooms, including a master bedroom with an attached bathroom and a big white bathtub gleamed inside. The rooms had big wardrobes, a dressing table with a long mirror and open cabinets overhead. Finally, the hall opened out into a capacious balcony.

Mohanaswamy's head began reeling. The attached toilet of the master bedroom alone was big enough for him to live a peaceful life, he thought. Why would he need any more space? All his clothes could be crammed into a single cupboard. Washing machine, fridge, microwave oven, geyser – he did not possess any of those appliances. He had never felt the need to buy them either. A small autorickshaw could hold the entirety of his belongings, so in which corner of this enormous flat would he arrange them? What would he – who enjoyed having food sitting on the floor and watching TV – do with those bulky sofas and armchairs? Who would use the dining table?

Mohanaswamy suddenly felt very small. Rajesh, playing the part of a seasoned salesman, went on describing the features of the flat. 'See, we have fixed grills to the balcony for children's safety. You can keep as big a bed as you want in the master bedroom. You can view the TV screen even from the kitchen. We have made this arrangement especially for the lady of the house, so that she won't get bored. If you want one or two more wardrobes, there is space for them as well. We have designed the building in such a way that neighbours cannot have even a small glimpse into your house. We believe in complete privacy for the family. Your balcony faces the children's playground. Sitting in the balcony you can watch your children play. We will give you two car parking slots…' Mohanaswamy was even more frightened now and he felt like running away from that place.

Pausing for a while, Rajesh asked, 'If you have anything particular in mind, please tell me, sir, we will get everything done. Tiles, wall colour, kitchen material, plywood, windows…'

Mohanaswamy had nothing to say. 'This is enough … it's nice. I don't want anything else. If you kindly let me know the amount to be paid as advance, I will write out a cheque today itself,' he said.

Now it was Rajesh's turn to be taken aback. 'Aiyoo … There is no urgency sir. Let your family too come and see the house. Let your children, parents, in-laws, all of them come and have a look first. Everyone will have their own preferences, right? Take a week's time sir, no problem. I will keep a flat reserved for you. If you rush into it, we may both land in trouble later,' Rajesh tried to convince him.

'Please, there is no need for all that. If I say okay, that's final. Please tell me how much I have to pay as advance,' Mohanaswamy urged.

Without trying to persuade further, Rajesh said, 'You will have to pay two lakh rupees as advance. The remaining thirty-eight lakhs can be paid at the time of registration. Registration charges will be separate.'

'And in whose name should the cheque be drawn?' Rajesh gave him a pamphlet, underlining the name of the company with a pen. Mohanaswamy hurriedly wrote out a cheque with trembling hands and handed it to Rajesh.

Rajesh was still a little puzzled and he didn't react for a while. Then he remembered his lines and shook Mohanaswamy's hands and said, 'Congratulations, sir! We will give you two air tickets to Singapore as a complementary gift. You can go there with your family for three days and two nights. Food and accommodation will be taken care of. You will get further details in a couple of days.'

Mohanaswamy did not say a word as Rajesh gave him an application form. 'Sir, please fill in all these columns,' he requested. Mohanaswamy ran his eyes over the page. There were more than fifty queries for customers relating to interiors: the choice of tiles, bathroom fittings, French windows, wall paint, cross-ventilation, TV cables, internet connection and so on. Certain choices would inflate the cost. At the end of the form, the house buyer had to put his signature.

Mohanaswamy neither had the interest nor the courage to answer those queries. He feared that if he stood there for some more time, he might collapse. He had made up his mind not to present himself as a lachrymose to Rajesh, a total stranger. But soon he sensed his determination crumbling, bit by bit. He did not tick any of the checkboxes, but simply signed off at the end of the form and returned it to Rajesh. 'You please fill it up for me. I'm not particular about all these things. Anything you say is okay. Don't worry about money, please,' he said. A bemused Rajesh simply nodded his head. 'Do I have to sign anywhere else?' Mohanaswamy enquired.

'No, sir, you will have to come back at the time of registration, that's enough. Please leave your mobile number and address.'

'I am going abroad tomorrow. My friend will help you in all these matters. I will give him the power of attorney. I will share his address and contact number. Is that okay?' he asked. Rajesh nodded.

Mohanaswamy rushed out of the apartment complex like a bat out of hell. The experience had been more harrowing than that endoscopy. He strongly felt that he should have had a low-paying job so that he would always be compelled to live in rented rooms. Will I be able to live in this big house once I return? He grew anxious. Whatever it is, one thing is for sure, I will not hold a house-warming ceremony. I swear, I won't do it! He said to himself repeatedly.

Rajesh stood in the balcony as he watched this strange fellow disappear into the dust, perplexed why he bought a house worth forty lakh rupees in just thirty minutes.

FOUR FACES

'Are you a Brahmin?' asked Darshan.

~

After Karthik left him, it took years for Mohanaswamy's wounds to heal. Getting his life on an even keel after the break-up wasn't easy. After all, Karthik was his first partner, who, after living in with him for a long time, went away and got married to a woman. It was a happy partnership which Mohanaswamy had believed would last a lifetime. But the painful separation left him completely bereft and changed his worldview about relationships. While he still searched for new companions to fulfil his sexual needs, he decided not to commit himself to long-term relationships. As a young man, people pestered him to get married, even offered to find him a bride. But when he came out of the closet, nobody had a heart large enough to advise him to find himself a boy and settle down. Mohanaswamy started living life the way he liked. In an uncaring society, who really gives a damn about you anyway?

As men walked into and out of his life one after the other, Mohanaswamy learnt to accept it all with the equanimity of a 'Sthitaprajna' – treating pleasure and pain alike. As he extended his connections with gay men, he saw a whole new exciting world opening before him. Every time Mohanaswamy made love to a new body, the experience was enchantingly different. The more he explored the more it got mysterious. And yet, as Mohanaswamy crossed forty-five, mental and emotional companionship became the more pressing need than lust. But he also knew that unless there was a physical involvement, people did not open up their mind and heart.

Mohanaswamy just couldn't forget Veluswamy, a twenty-five-year-old whom he met through Grindr, a gay dating app. The picture of his athletic physique turned on Mohanaswamy. At the same time, he was sceptical whether such a handsome young man would oblige a middle-aged man like him. Also he wasn't sure whether he would be able to keep up with Veluswamy's in bed. But Veluswamy's stunning looks drew him like magnet. He decided to try his luck and sent him a 'hello'.

The relationship progressed as any other – long chats on the internet, a cup of coffee at Costa, a movie at the multiplex and a meal at Pizza Hut – and within a week, Mohanaswamy succeeded in bringing Veluswamy home. But he still wasn't sure whether Veluswamy had any interest in him. Is this young man really interested in me? Or has he come to my house purely out of respect for my age? Mohanaswamy's mind reeled under the fear of rejection. But he tried to hide his anxiety. They had dinner together and nattered on about this and that for a while. Finally, when it was time to sleep, Mohanaswamy asked him hesitatingly, 'Do you prefer sleeping in a separate room or will you sleep with me in my bedroom?'

Veluswamy, who had sensed his anxiety all along, smiled, and suddenly pulled him closer and passionately kissed him on the lips, igniting flames of desire in him. Unable to hold out any longer, Mohanaswamy took Veluswamy's clothes off greedily.

It wasn't a smooth ride, though. As Mohanaswamy frenziedly went for his stark naked body, Veluswamy stopped him. 'Sir, I want to tell you something before we proceed,' he said.

Mohanaswamy was irked. It was like being intercepted

by a traffic cop when you were on a joy ride. Even then, he exercised restraint and asked, 'What?'

'Sir, I am HIV positive. I came to know about it a year ago. Now I am on medication. I am telling this to you in advance because I don't want to be dishonest,' he said calmly.

Veluswamy's disclosure came as a bolt from the blue. Mohanaswamy took a step back.

Noticing his uneasiness, Veluswamy reiterated, 'I could have hidden it from you. But sir, you see, I did not want to be dishonest.'

Mohanaswamy was moved by his honesty, but still he hesitated to proceed.

Veluswamy continued, 'Sir, you are well educated, and I expect you to be in the know of things. I have condoms with me. Don't worry, nothing will happen,' he said in an assuring tone.

Mohanaswamy couldn't help but give into his persuasions, mad as he was over the young man's winsome looks. He had read a lot about HIV and the knowledge gave him the courage. Then there was no stopping them as they hungrily devoured each other's bodies.

Veluswamy woke up at the break of the dawn. He planted a light kiss on Mohanaswamy's sleepy eyes and murmured, 'I love your courage, sir.' He then put his clothes on, wrapped the condoms carefully in a piece of paper, discarded them in the dustbin and left. A contended Mohanaswamy lay swooning in the bed till well after sunrise. But finally when he got up, sunlight had lit up the room and the terrible reality dawned upon him. Will I too get HIV? he shuddered. His mind was swirling with the niggling thought as he brushed his teeth, took his bath and offered puja to the gods.

He did not feel like going to office and applied for leave via email. He forced himself to have breakfast and rushed to Victoria Hospital, overwrought. The hospital had an exclusive unit to screen gay men for HIV. He had been there a few times before for routine check-up and had come out with a smiling face. But this time it was different. Anxiety was writ large on his face. 'Why did I get into bed with Veluswamy knowing his HIV status?' he cursed himself under his breath. Condoms, he thought, may not be a hundred per cent foolproof. A drop of semen – that too of a robust young man – would have lakhs of sperms in it, rushing with immense force. How could a condom – after all a small rubber pouch – contain it all? Mohanaswamy was assailed by these scary thoughts.

When he expressed his concerns to the lady doctor at the hospital, she just laughed it off. 'You have read so much about HIV. And you used condoms, right? Then why are you so vexed?' she said, brushing aside his worries. But theory is often far from reality, thought Mohanaswamy. Seeing him still anxious, the doctor said, 'If it still bothers you, take the test. But the presence of the virus will be known only after three months.'

'Three months! What will I do till then?' cried Mohanaswamy.

'Use condoms without fail,' she said.

Those three months were nothing short of hell for Mohanaswamy. An unutterable sadness enveloped him. Even a small fluctuation in health gave him the jitters. How a tiny virus, hard to detect even under the microscope, had ruined a wise Mohanaswamy's days and nights! 'Oh! To hell with me! Why did I knowingly invite this trouble? Why did I allow myself to fall for the desire?' he wailed.

Veluswamy continued sending him messages on WhatsApp. 'Sir, shall we meet again, please? It's very difficult to find brave people like you. What a pleasure it was to be with you! The memories thrill me till date. We shall meet again, sir, please,' he texted, enclosing an emoji of two men holding hands.

But Mohanaswamy had no courage to meet Veluswamy again. He made excuses to avoid him. 'If you too start acting like others, where will I go, sir? Should HIV positive people be deprived of sexual pleasure all their life? We too have physical needs like you all,' he sent a message along with a crying-face emoji.

But Mohanaswamy was unmoved. Thereafter there were no messages from him.

On the day that marked the completion of the three restless months, Mohanaswamy ran to Victoria Hospital to know the results of the HIV test. 'It's negative,' said the lady doctor with a smile. 'You were unnecessarily worried.' The news came as a big relief to Mohanaswamy. All his worries vanished into thin air. He emerged triumphant from the hospital with a broad smile, went straight to a corner ice-cream shop and relished a huge honey dew. He felt on top of the world.

But as his anxiety disappeared, physical desire raised its head again. Veluswamy's hot body began hovering before his eyes. Not that he wouldn't get anyone else. But his mind was obsessed with Veluswamy – his honesty, his strong body and tender age. His gentle kiss on the eyes and murmured words of love. Temptation surged through him at the thought of the night spent with Veluswamy. If a condom – just a tiny rubber pouch – can prevent all ills, why succumb to fear? Why stop bedding such a wonderful fellow just because of some petty virus? Besides, hadn't he read up enough new articles and stories on the internet about gays living happily with HIV positive people?

'Shall we meet this weekend?' Mohanaswamy texted Veluswamy, enclosing a red-lips emoji. There was no reply from him for a couple of days. However, a text came on the third day: 'My health is giving me problems, sir. I can't meet you for a few months'.

'What happened to you, Velu? Aren't you taking your pills?' Mohanaswamy asked in concern.

'HIV is under control, sir, that's not a problem. But these days I am coughing a lot. Doctors suspect it to be tuberculosis. HIV diminishes our immunity, making it easy for harmful microbes to thrive in our body. I have lost 10 kgs in three months,' he replied.

Mohanaswamy was sad. 'So what? We can still meet. Why don't you come over?' he said, trying to cheer him up.

'Sir, HIV is a simple infection which can be prevented by using a condom. But is there a contraceptive for TB? No, there isn't any. There is no point in meeting now,' he replied.

After that, Mohanaswamy decided not to disturb him.

~

Ramadhar Trivedi hailed from Varanasi. Born into a pandit family, he grew up swimming in the river Ganga and practising yoga that his grandfather had taught him. He could bend and twist his body like rubber. He had a slim waistline and a tall, lean body like a eucalyptus tree. He was just two years younger to Mohanaswamy, but looked much younger. Mohanaswamy was enamoured of his expressive eyes and the dimples on his cheeks. Ramadhar was a man of few words. He spoke like a scholar, weighing out every word. He had studied Sanskrit at the Banaras Hindu University. He religiously applied vibhuti on his forehead and kumkum between his eyebrows. He earned his living as a yoga teacher. He went to software engineers' houses in Bengaluru and taught them yoga. Since he belonged to the priest class, people sometimes requested him to perform puja at their houses. Both these occupations earned him good money though money was his least concern. 'I had never thought that the yoga and the mantras I learnt during my childhood would one day help me earn my keep,' he would tell Mohanaswamy modestly.

Though Ramadhar Trivedi was physically robust, he had feminine traits. Until a few years ago, Mohanaswamy had never felt attracted to effiminate men. His choice would always be the rough and tough alpha male types. But now he was mature enough to accept people as they were. Moreover, when Ramadhar took Mohanaswamy to bed, he was out-and-out masculine. The energy with which he rode him till late midnight without any signs of tiredness awed Mohanaswamy. What was the source of his unflagging vigour? Was it the river Ganga where he swam regularly or the yoga which he practiced so rigorously? Mohanaswamy wondered. Perhaps only Lord Vishwanatha of Varanasi knew the secret.

Ramadhar was a mature person, calm and poised at all times. Mohanaswamy had never heard him complaining about life. As a yoga teacher, he rode his bike long distances every day going to software engineers' houses in different parts of the city, but never cribbed about traffic jams. He was very punctual, always reaching his destination on time. He never skipped the three-time sandhyavandana, doing it with religious fervour. He meditated, studied Sanskrit and religious texts most part of the day and hardly talked about sex. His unflappability often irritated Mohanaswamy.

At the beginning of their relationship, Ramadhar put a condition. 'When two persons start living in, it is as good as marriage. A marriage won't be successful unless the couple are loyal to each other. If you are loyal to me, I can live happily with you. On my part, I promise you, I will never jump the fence,' he said. Mohanaswamy was glad in a way. Settling down with Ramadhar seemed a better option than hunting for new faces all the time. He agreed happily.

Everything went well for some time. Mohanaswamy was at the peak of joy. Those were the days of immense happiness. Ramadhar moved in with him. He kept the house clean and tidy, doing all the chores himself. He was a good cook and prepared north Indian delicacies. Mohanaswamy relished all the food and attention he got. He became lazy and also put on some weight. But a fitness freak, he soon brought himself on back on track, going for brisk walks and a trek to the Himalayas to shed calories.

Ramadhar kept his words and showed unflinching devotion to Mohanaswamy. Sometimes when they walked together on the streets, Mohanaswamy would point to handsome young men around and exclaim, 'Wow! So hot!' But Ramadhar would just smile. He was never inclined towards other men. Even in bed, he carried himself with the same poise, at an unhurried pace, without ever getting tired. 'The union of two bodies is akin to yoga,' he would explain. 'We must become one with each other without any haste or stress, just like a fish swimming quietly in the Ganga at dusk.' In stripping, hugging, kissing, stroking or ejaculating, he had the art of beginning it at a slow pace and taking it to a high pitch, like singers do in Hindustani classical music. According to him, the satisfaction one derived from climbing the mountain in Tirupati barefoot and seeking the darshan of Lord Thimmappa after standing in a long queue, could not be found in whizzing up the mountain in a swanky car and entering the temple directly through the VIP route, skipping the queue. He would give many such examples to stress the power of dedication and equanimity.

But soon Mohanaswamy began finding it all too boring. Sex with Ramadhar, though still pleasurable, was losing its novelty. Mohanaswamy wanted sex on tap, any time with anyone of his choice. Just go to the internet and you will find plenty of good-looking boys. Open the Grindr app on your mobile and it will throw up responses from hot, dashing men, one of whom could be living only a stone's throw away from your house. When the world was filled with such beautiful possibilities, why cling to a single partner? Better to break up with one and take up with another. Then another. In variety was spice, Mohanaswamy was convinced, and a monotonous life with just one partner was nothing but a state of inertia.

But no such thoughts seemed to perturb Ramadhar. He was the same, calm and composed, living with unswerving loyalty to Mohanaswamy. His composure irritated Mohanaswamy even more and soon he began resenting Ramadhar's presence. Earlier he was free as a flying bird, but now Ramadhar had clipped his wings. He got sick of the banality of everyday life. This was not how he had wanted it. But he could not say it directly. The bottled up anger and frustration soon began finding different outlets. Bickering became quite common and differences began to surface. Mohanaswamy often nagged Ramadhar over his overtly religious behaviour. 'You know how our religious leaders and pontiffs join hands in opposing our clan. Still, why are you so obsessed with religion?' he would taunt Ramadhar.

To this, Ramadhar would calmly reply, 'If you had studied religion deeply you wouldn't be making such statements. There is no point in arguing with people with half knowledge.'

But Mohanaswamy wouldn't stop picking on him. 'These north Indians love fighting. They cannot simply get along with us south Indians,' he would say querulously. Ramadhar would ignore it as if it was not directed at him and get on with his chores. But Mohanaswamy wouldn't leave it at that. 'You are also a north Indian. Do I take your silence as an endorsement of my view?'

To this Ramadhar would calmly reply, 'Wherever you go in this world there are both good and bad people, be it south India or north India.'

All in all, Mohanaswamy's patience was waning. He suffered like a patient on a strict dietary regimen. It was during those days that he happened to meet Shantanu Biswas. It was Vaikuntha Ekadashi and Ramadhar had forcibly taken him to Venkateshwara temple. The temple was teeming with people. As they stood in a line for the lord's darshan, a man approached Ramadhar and called him aside, saying, 'Guruji, I want to discuss the matter of my daughter's matrimony with you.' As Ramadhar went following that gentleman, Mohanaswamy's eyes rested on the married man standing right in front of him in the queue, carrying his crying baby on his shoulder. He had removed his t-shirt and wrapped it around his waist as men were not allowed inside the temple with their shirts on. Mohanaswamy had observed that newly married men with a baby had a certain charm in them. They are neither like a blossoming bud nor like a withering flower. Rather, they look like full-blown flowers ablaze in the morning sun. They often put on a little weight after marriage, a sign of a happy content life.

Pushing their way across the press of people, Mohanaswamy and Shantanu felt each other's bodies and flames of desire shot through them. They took no time to find out that both their needs were the same. Mohanaswamy gently caressed the baby's cheeks and asked, 'What's your name, sweetie?' On the pretext of taking the little boy from the father's arms, Mohanaswamy's hand touched Shantanu's hairy chest. Shantanu did not object. In fact, he responded warmly, leaning in on Mohanaswamy at every pretext while standing in the queue. Mohanaswamy marvelled at the way lust prevails over man with least regard for time and space. Even when you stand in the temple, folding your hands before god, you may, without a pinch of guilt, enjoy sensual pleasure from a body pressing from behind.

By the time they came out of the temple, they had exchanged their mobile numbers. Shantanu's Tamil wife, who had gone to get the sacred rice, came back after a while and took the baby from her husband's arms.

Earlier, Mohanaswamy would bring boys home boldly, without having to give any explanation to anybody. But now he could not do so as he feared Ramadhar finding out. He considered going to Shantanu's house. Shantanu worked from home two days a week and his wife three days a week, to look after their child. They both were software engineers. They earned handsome salaries and lived in a luxury apartment on the fourteenth floor. Mohanaswamy liked their spacious house. But he felt somewhat guilty about these secret meetings. He found the couple's one-year-old son to be a problem. Sometimes, when Mohanaswamy and Shantanu lay in bed, the little boy would come crawling, playing with his Lego toys and trying to stand up holding on to the bed. 'Honey, please go now,' Shantanu would plead. Sometimes, the baby would start crying and a naked Shantanu would run around the house looking for the feeding bottle as Mohanaswamy sat watching the entire scene helplessly.

By the time Shantanu came back, Mohanaswamy's zeal would have fizzled out.

Then there was one more problem. Right in front of the bed, on the wall, there was a photo framing Shantanu with his wife and kid. Mohanaswamy's eyes would fall on it every time he had sex with Shantanu. The photo reminded him of Shantanu's happy married life. As did the food kept in the kitchen, the shampoo bottles and soaps lined up in the bathroom, baby diapers lying in the bedroom, the pillow covers with 'I Love You' embroidered on them and the doormat outside the house that read 'Welcome' – all triggering a sense of guilt in him. He sometimes wondered why Shantanu, who had such a loving family, craved for another body. One day, just before leaving, he asked Shantanu directly.

Shantanu wasn't expecting this question. He sat down on the edge of the bed, looking down at his toes, not knowing what to say.

'I am sorry,' Mohanaswamy said wistfully, stroking his shoulders.

'You like to make love only to men. And so does my wife. You both see the world with the same eyes. But for me it is not so simple. My body craves for both male and female bodies. Unless I have them both, I feel incomplete. My parents washed their hands off after getting me married. But for me, it is only half the meal.

What do I do? I haven't done any injustice to her. I love her a lot. And right from rinsing the baby's bum to driving the car for the family, I do everything for them. Tell me, what else can I do? Are you trying to tell me that I should deprive my body of its needs? Aren't you being cruel?' he asked, tears in his eyes.

Mohanaswamy felt sorry for him. 'Take it easy. I didn't mean to hurt you,' he said softly.

It wasn't long before that their relationship ran its course. In fact, Mohanaswamy knew from the very beginning that it would not last long. Married men are always obsessed with their families. And if they have kids, it is very difficult to catch them especially on the weekends. But if their wives go to their parents' place for a holiday, these men will be after their gay friends, pleading them to come home. And they will plunder all they can in that short period. And if their wives call when they are in bed with their gay friends, they will mumble, 'Yes honey ... I am at home ... playing with the baby ... Miss you ... Please come soon ... Love you ... Hug you.' When they reeled out lie after lie, Mohanaswamy just hated it.

Mohanaswamy had observed how a once handsome groom became lazy after marriage. His wife and her family members put him on the pedestal. Since he took his wife for granted to fulfill all his physical and other needs, he did not care to maintain his body and soon ran into fat. Mohanaswamy thought of his former partner Karthik, who, once so handsome, had now become so unattractive that Mohanaswamy could not fancy him even in his dreams. Even Karthik's wife, he concluded, may not be allowing her plump, middle-aged husband to come near her. Shantanu Biswas too was on the same course. His cheeks were swelling and his tummy was showing. 'You better start going to the gym, Shantanu, or at least go for brisk walks,' Mohanaswamy advised him a couple of times to which Shantanu just nodded.

And then, one day, the unthinkable happened. That evening, after making love, Mohanaswamy and Shantanu fell fast asleep, knowing for sure that Shantanu's wife would come back from office only after 9 p.m. The child also went off to sleep. Suddenly the door bell rang. 'Mohana, please go and see who is at the door. It must be the newspaper boy asking for money. Just tell him to come tomorrow…' Shantanu pleaded lazily. Mohanaswamy got up reluctantly, wrapped a towel around his waist and went to open the door. He was startled to see Ramadhar at the door. Ramadhar with the vibhuti on his forehead, a dab of kumkum between his eyebrows, dressed in white and a helmet in his hand. His eyes glistened with tears. Though not so sad himself, Mohanaswamy felt sorry for Ramadhar. And he did not know how to square it with him. 'I am sorry,' he stammered, stepped forward to stroke Ramadhar's hair.

'Don't touch me, please,' Ramadhar said loudly with a sullen face. By then Shantanu came out from the bedroom. He was at a loss.

'Ram guru, please come inside. He is my close friend, Mohanaswamy,' he said, putting his hands around Mohanaswamy's bare shoulders. Embarrassed, Mohanaswamy took Shantanu's hands off his shoulders. 'Mohana, meet my friend, Ramadhar, a very good yoga teacher. You were insisting that I should lose weight, right? So I have appointed him. He will now be coming to my house twice a week to teach me yoga. You too can join in if you are interested...' he went on.

Ramadhar stormed out and ran downstairs. 'Guruji, why are you going back?' Shantanu cried, running after Ramadhar.

The baby woke up to the noise and started crying. 'Don't cry, my boy. Your father will come back soon,' Mohanaswamy tried to console the child.

Darshan was dark-skinned, just like Lord Krishna, Mohanaswamy's favourite deity. In the photo on the dating app he looked dashing – a broad chest without hair, dark nipples, deep navel, narrow waist, strong arms, a lovable face, straight nose and shining eyes. The stone stud in his right ear and the copper bracelet on his right forearm suited him well. The low rise jeans revealed his red underwear, taking Mohanaswamy's breath away.

The first couple of months after the unedifying experience at Shantanu's house, Mohanaswamy was quite upset. At the same time, he was relieved to be out of Ramadhar's grip. But it was not so easy to forget Ramadhar and the good care he had taken of him. He recalled the sufferings he went through after Karthik ditched him. Now he himself had ditched a good companion mercilessly and also had the stone-heart to justify it. As the guilt pierced him, he sent a 'sorry' message to Ramadhar. He also tried ringing him up. But Ramadhar did not reply. People who live life on their own terms are adamant. And they can never be happy. Concluding so, Mohanaswamy decided to forget about him.

At the same time, Shantanu did not get any closer to him. Shantanu's needs were only physical. His mind always revolved around his family and Mohanaswamy knew that a physical relationship without mental bonding would not last long. He lost interest in going to Shantanu's place. Once or twice, he invited Shantanu to come over to his house, but Shantanu did not agree as he had to bring his son along, who was growing up, saying a few words by then. Worse, he had learnt to click photos on his father's mobile. What if something untoward happened and his wife found them out?

It was around then that he met Darshan.

Darshan was in his thirties. Mohanaswamy sent him long messages extolling his physique. Strangely, there was no reply. Not ready to accept rejection, Mohanaswamy sent him another lengthy message after two days. Again, there was no reply.

'Any problem?' Mohanaswamy asked.

'No English,' pat came the reply.

'Kannadadavana?' Mohanaswamy typed in Kannada text, asking if he was a Kannadiga.

Darshan was very happy. 'Are you also a Kannadiga? I don't know English well. Here everybody speaks English,' he replied in Kannada, using English font.

Now Mohanaswamy understood his problem. Most dating apps use an English language interface, the users are also expected to communicate in English. People who developed them didn't seem to have given any thought to making them user-friendly for non-English-language users who are comfortable only in the vernacular. Mohanaswamy wondered how in this modern world, only those who knew English thrived. And that included gays.

Thereafter Darshan sent message after message in Kannada using English font. Once during a chat, he asked, '*Maga, Neenu hasigenyage keytiya illa keysikoltiya*?' In bed, will you be fucking me or will you get fucked?

Mohanaswamy blushed coyly as he was not used to gay slang in Kannada. In English, its equivalent was 'top or bottom?' but the Kannada phrase sounded funny. He too replied in Kannada. Darshan was very happy. 'In that case, I am sure we will make a happy pair,' he texted.

They decided to go out for dinner. Since Darshan was a non-vegetarian and Mohanaswamy was a vegetarian they decided to go to Nagarjuna, an Andhra-style restaurant. Darshan came in gaudy clothes and cooling glasses. He is perhaps not used to going to hotels, Mohanaswamy thought. Without even going through the menu, Mohanaswamy placed order for a vegetarian thali while Darshan ordered mutton biriyani. It was then that Darshan asked him, 'Are you a Brahmin?'

'No Darshan, a gay belongs to no caste. People from no caste or community will accept him within their fold,' he said.

Darshan readily agreed to come to Mohanaswamy's house. On the way he asked, 'Do you live alone?'

'Yes, of course,' Mohanaswamy said. 'What about you?'

'I am not yet married. But my mother insists that I should get married. I don't know what to do, I don't fancy women very much. Even though fucking them shouldn't be a problem...'

Mohanaswamy laughed heartily at this. 'Darshan, marriage is not all about sex. It is the union of two persons living together. Can you live with a woman all your life?'

Pondering over it for a moment, Darshan said, 'To be honest, I haven't fucked a single woman so far in life. But if it comes to that, I think I can do it. Look here. See my strength,' he pushed up the sleeves of his shirt and displayed his biceps.

Mohanaswamy laughed. Consumed with desire, he gently ran his fingers over the Scorpio tattoo on his upper arm and exclaimed, 'Super!' Then he added, 'But Darshan, think twice before you take a decision. After all it's the question of someone else's life too.'

When he unlocked the door, it was dark. Two hungry bodies met on that cold winter night. Mohanaswamy, who had tasted many bodies, found Darshan's towering aggression somewhat special. His hot breath, his virility, his perfect moves – his vigour seemed to be so natural, not something acquired artificially in a gym. Mohanaswamy considered it was his sheer luck that he ran into Darshan. For him Darshan was like a Gandharva, a heavenly being, descending from the world of Manmatha, the Lord of Love.

When Darshan loosened his grip, it was past midnight. Bathed in sweat and tired, Mohanaswamy exulted in pain and pleasure. He switched on the fan and its cool air made the hair on his body stand on its end. 'Thank you,' he whispered into Darshan's ears. Darshan smiled. Mohanaswamy kissed him on the chest and got up from the bed. As he walked towards the bathroom, he stepped on his undergarments which lay on the floor. 'You monster … you big monster,' he said flirtatiously, throwing them at Darshan. He then switched on the lights and went to the bathroom.

When he came back, Darshan was sitting on the bed glumly, separating Mohanaswamy's janivara, the sacred thread, tangled in his vest. His eyes were wet and he looked vexed.

'What happened, Darshan?' Mohanaswamy asked.

'Why did you lie to me? I asked you whether you are a Brahmin…' he said, tears in his eyes.

'How does that matter, Darshan? I don't attach any significance to my caste.'

'Then why do you wear this janivara?'

'That is because my sister often conducts family functions at the Raghavendra Swami temple. Wearing the janivara is a must for men at such religious places. Otherwise they don't serve us food. And I don't want to upset my family for something this petty. So I just wear this because I don't know when I will need it. Except this, the janivara holds no significance for me,' he asserted.

'But you were born into a house of Brahmins, right?'

'Yes. But how does it matter?'

'It matters. Because if I sleep with Brahmins, I will be incurring their wrath. They will curse me.'

'Who told you all this, Darshan?'

'My mother,' he sighed.

Mohanaswamy did not know how to handle the situation. He just sat besides Darshan, caressing his back. 'Relax, Darshan,' he said.

'My name is Madesha ... not Darshan. I come from a village near Chamarajnagar.'

Mohanaswamy quietly nodded his head, allowing him to speak.

'I am from a lower caste. My father was working at the house of a Brahmin family. They were good people. They took good care of us. But a young, married woman of the family, who came back as a widow at an early age, was drawn to my father, who was so very good looking. She trapped him despite his resistance. Thereafter a curse befell our family. My sister, who was engaged to get married in a couple of months, died of a mysterious disease. My mother fell ill. Possessed by some ghost, she would wake up in the middle of the night and beat my father black and blue. I don't know what went wrong, one day my father's body was found floating in a well. People in the town told us that the Brahmins' curse made it all happen. I did not feel like living there any longer. I came to the city in search of livelihood as nobody would give me a job in that goddamned village. But before I left, my mother warned me not to sleep with any Brahmin girl as it would only do me harm. I promised her I would not. Now she is also not well, she is counting her days. And then I have this bloody habit of sleeping with men. I think this too is a curse from the Brahmins,' he said with a heavy sigh.

Mohanaswamy was clueless as to how to react to abstruse story, full of unfounded beliefs and superstitions. If he dismissed it outright, he knew he would be hurting Darshan.

'Hey, Darsan!' he said.

'Not Darshan. I am Madesha…' he corrected him.

'Madesha, don't be silly. I don't possess the power either to curse you or to gift you with a boon. Anyway, you had promised your mother that you would not sleep with Brahmin women, right? But I am not a woman, I am a man. So where is the question of a curse?'

'But how does it make any difference, magaa? When I touch someone sexually, whether a boy or a girl, it makes no difference. Tell me, why did you hide the fact that you are a Brahmin?' he wailed.

'If you are so scared about the curse, do one thing. In the living room outside, there is a photo of Lord Venkataramana hanging on the wall. Go and fold your hands before him. God is bigger than everyone. He will forgive all sins.'

This seemed to appeal to Madesha. He slowly got up from the bed, wore his clothes and staggered out of the room. Mohanaswamy followed him and switched on the light in the hall. Madesha folded his hands before Lord Venkataramana. He then turned to Mohanaswamy and said, 'Please don't send me any more messages. I don't want to sleep with Brahmins.'

Then he walked out of the house.

MT KILIMANJARO

We decided to begin the last leg of the trek to Mount Kilimanjaro at the stroke of midnight on the fourth day. On the first three days, the climb began in the mornings but suddenly they were switching to midnight. Mohanaswamy was vexed. 'This trail is not like the previous ones, my child. It is steeper and narrower. It is best if you don't see what you are climbing, or you will be too scared to continue. Since visibility is extremely low at night, you will not get as frightened. If you see it in the morning, you will not even dare go near it,' David explained.

It was a pitch-dark amavasya night. 'Light scares you, but night gives you courage.' David had put forth this weird logic, as they stood at 4,730 metres altitude. What they perceive to be the truth is probably different here in Tanzania, Mohanaswamy thought to himself. 'Just follow my steps, my child. I will ensure that you reach the summit at the break of dawn,' David tried to boost him. The huge, tall and dark Maasai guide was in his early fifties and took liberty of calling Mohanaswamy 'my child'. Mohanaswamy did not object to this display of familial affection as it came from a rough and tough looking man like David. In fact, this paradox of toughness and tenderness surprised him.

A numbing cold had enveloped the dark, gloomy night. Mohanaswamy's equally gloomy mind was swimming with intrusive thoughts. It is said that this ice-topped Kilimanjaro Mountain, rising from the desert planes, hides a fire in its womb. While these volcanic cones have not erupted in recent history, they could explode anytime! It suddenly seemed to him that the gigantic mountain was just waiting to spew lava. From its outer appearance nobody could judge its inner turmoil. These days, when outer appearances matter the most, who has the patience to dig inside hearts?

During dinner that night, his teammates were enthusiastically discussing the temperature. While one said it was minus ten degree Celsius, another argued it could be minus eight. Mohanaswamy was too jittery to participate in any of these discussions. David had served them noodles, but he couldn't eat more than two mouthfuls. A throbbing headache and nausea was draining him out. 'Oxygen levels are extremely low at this altitude, my child. Your body is struggling because it has not adapted to the changed atmosphere. But don't worry. The body has immense power, it acclimatizes itself with all sorts of climatic conditions. But you must prepare your body by eating well. Without strength, how will you accomplish this uphill task?' David gently tried persuading him to eat some more.

'No, I just can't bear to consume a single morsel…' Mohanaswamy pushed his plate aside.

'Then you must at least drink a glass of milk,' David urged.

By the time he finished drinking the milk, he saw David with the cook and the porter, sitting around the fire, hogging the leftover noodles like they hadn't eaten in days. Poverty is cruel. He pitied these Maasai men as he observed them polishing off whatever was left on the plates after the climbers had eaten. Unable to bear the unpleasant sight, he returned to his hut.

There were three huts, each one accommodating about twenty people on bunk beds. They had been served dinner as early as seven in the evening and were urged to sleep for a few hours before being woken up at midnight for the summit trek. Mohanaswamy could not sleep. He looked around. A young American couple slept cosily in a sleeping bag, snuggled into each other's arms. An Italian gay couple fell silent after much squirming on the bed. In the far corner, an elderly couple from Denmark was fast asleep. A college student from England slept soundly on a bed on the other side. Their snoring filled the hut. There was absolutely no noise outside. No animals can live in Kilimanjaro as they cannot survive the extreme climatic conditions. Kilimanjaro is so lonely! It conceals the blazing fire in its womb while masquerading as a cold, icy mountain.

Mohanaswamy found himself pondering over his decision to climb the mountain. Why did I embark on this journey? Now I have landed in this strange land, surrounded by strangers. Why was I overwhelmingly driven by the word 'Kilimanjaro'? Maybe I just wanted to escape from my mundane world. How delusional I'd been! Why was I so keen to summit Kilimanjaro even before I saw the Himalayas? Mohanaswamy tossed and turned on the bed. Soon it will be 11.30 and David will come to wake me up. I have to get up and go. I have to ascend the peak. There's no escape. I'm helpless. I'm vulnerable. There is no way to avoid it. I have to keep going. Nothing ceases to move. Nothing reaches its destination. What the poet Kuvempu said is perhaps right.

~

They walked in the path of the light from the torches strapped to their foreheads. David took the lead and Mohanaswamy followed him, anxiety written all over his face. The two other boys did not want to come. They said they would stay back at the base and take care of Mohanaswamy's luggage. Thwack … thwack … thwack … David hit the path with his stick as he marched ahead. Mohanaswamy followed the sound, placing his feet carefully in David's wake. Even in real life there should have been someone to show me the path, guarding me through each and every step like this, Mohanaswamy thought. How could David negotiate the switchbacks so effortlessly in the dark? How did he know the slopes and bends so well? 'Kilimanjaro is my home, my child. Here I can walk around anytime, even at night,' David said with a laugh, almost as if he could read Mohanaswamy's thoughts. He had climbed the mountain countless times.

With trekking poles in their hands, Mohanaswamy put one foot after the next making way through the sand and rock fragments. In some places, the rocks were capped with snow. Melting snow water mixed with sand filled the crevices between the rocks, emanating a strange smell. Stars filled the sky above. Mohanaswamy had not seen so many of them before. The air became thinner and oxygen levels dipped as they moved up. Mohanaswamy found himself gasping for breath and his thoughts strayed to philosophical musings yet again. When we are on the earth, we never realize the importance of oxygen. Abundance breeds contempt. Mohanaswamy felt that this extended to life, and we should never be easily available to anyone, lest we are taken for granted.

Air pressure decreased with each arduous step forward. Exhausted, Mohanaswamy sat down on the rocks every now and then, wishing time away. David would stop too, giving him water or peppermint.

'David, tell me, after this painstaking journey what do we get to see from the peak?' Mohanaswamy asked.

'Nothing, my child. It is the summit point of Kilimanjaro, Africa's highest peak, that's all.'

'In our country, there will normally be a temple on top of the hill, so that after climbing with so much difficulty, people can have a vision of god. You people should also set up a temple there.'

David was silent for a while. Mohanaswamy gasped and wished he hadn't asked the question. But David slowly said, 'For us Kilimanjaro Mountain itself is the god. Why do we need another temple?'

David's statements often left Mohanaswamy nonplussed. Whenever Mohanaswamy, by force of habit, drew comparisons between the customs and practices in India and those prevailing in the rest of the world, David would stun him with unexpected answers. A similar episode had taken place the previous day. When they started from Horombo Hut, the porter and the cook, followed them carrying Mohanaswamy's fifteen kilo bag full of clothes and other essentials and another heavy bag with the cooking stove, some utensils and groceries. David carried Mohanaswamy's small backpack containing dry food, water and coffee. They were to be paid a few dollars for their services, the lion's share of which would go to David and the remaining small amount to be distributed evenly between the other two.

'In our Himalayas, donkeys are used for carrying luggage. Why don't you all do the same here? Why do you exert yourselves like this?' Mohanaswamy asked.

'In that case, we will have to spend half our wages on feeding the donkeys. What do we eat then?' David had snubbed him with his instant response.

Mohanaswamy became silent. The image of the trio stuffing their faces with leftover food at the mess floated unbidden before his eyes and turned his stomach. Unfamiliar terrains lay bare our personal weaknesses and faults. That's why that we must travel. Mountains allow us to transform ourselves, to face realities and admit our vulnerabilities. They kill our ego and make us humble, Mohanaswamy's mind wandered.

That night, the porter and the cook came to collect their wages. Handing them the dollar bills, Mohanaswamy probed, 'Why don't you both become guides like David? You can also earn more like him.'

'No English, no dollar … donkey, donkey…' the porter said, braying and flapping his palms behind his ears. Mohanaswamy did not know whether to laugh or cry at this gesture. But the cook had a good belly laugh.

'Get up, my child. Let's start. We should be at the summit before sunrise,' David alerted him. Mohanaswamy rose reluctantly and started dragging his feet. Before the sun's rays begin to poke through the clouds and turn the spotlight on the pitfalls of my life, I must finish my journey up to the destination through this inky night. A hundred salutes to darkness!

Before beginning his summit bid, Mohanaswamy had bundled himself in multiple layers of clothing – three pairs of trousers, four shirts, a pullover, three pairs of socks and two pairs of gloves. He had wrapped a muffler around his face, worn a monkey cap on top and strapped a head lamp to his forehead. Buckling under the weight of his clothing, Mohanaswamy found it difficult to bend and put on his hiking boots. David helped him out by sitting at his feet and tying the laces. Strangely, David hadn't put on so many layers of clothing – he just wore his jeans, a shirt, a pullover and a coat. He wore thick socks and no boots, only a pair of chappals.

'Don't you feel the need to protect yourself in warm clothes?' Mohanaswamy asked him.

'Kilimanjaro is like my mother. She will always protect me,' David said, smiling.

Mohanaswamy had started the climb much before the others as he was not able to sleep. With each step, he felt dog-tired and dizzy, stricken by altitude sickness. Fear churned inside him as he sweated under the thick cover of clothes. He wanted to stop and sit back every five minutes, but David had begun to give serious instructions. He didn't allow him to sit and instead urged him to relax for a few seconds while standing. Mohanaswamy gazed up at the last trail he would ascend and all he could see was a line of small bright headlights going up the mountain under the star-studded sky. It was as if an entire galaxy had descended on the earth. He looked back to see some hikers trailing behind him at a distance with lights attached to their foreheads.

'Why did you come alone, my child? You should have brought a friend or companion along with you,' David said.

Mohanaswamy did not reply. He turned his head and saw the flashlights slowly approaching him. In a while, they would all move past him. He would be left behind. Well, it was he who was depleted of energy, not them. It was he who came to this unknown world all alone, not them. They were also exhausted like him but not devoid of hope. They also walked in the dark like him but unlike him, they did not suffer from crippling feelings of loneliness.

'Water…' he pleaded. David came a few steps back and poured hot water from the flask into a cup. They both took a few sips. Then Mohanaswamy began vomiting. He threw up whatever little noodles he had eaten for dinner. He sank to the ground, almost on the verge of tears. David came rushing and caressed his back. 'Take care, my child, relax.'

Three separate lights came near them. It was the pair from Italy and their guide. 'What happened?' they asked. One of the couple advised him to have a piece of chocolate. 'Honey, please give him a chocolate,' the guy told his partner who promptly fished out a candy from his waist pouch and handed it to Mohanaswamy. 'Hakunamatata,' they said before leaving, a Swahili phrase which they had picked up during the expedition, which roughly meant 'don't worry'. Other flashlights joined them soon, leaving Mohanaswamy where he was.

Nobody waits for anybody. Everyone has their own path and destination.

'Be fast, my child, we still have to climb one thousand metres. We don't have much time,' David urged him. Dead on his feet, Mohanaswamy staggered on. The chocolate tasted bitter in his mouth after those bouts of vomiting and nausea.

'If you want to be a successful trekker you must bear one thing in mind, my child. Come what may, never back off. Never allow negative thoughts to waver your mind. Never consider descending before reaching your destination. No matter how tired you are, compose yourself and keep going. It is not enough to have a strong body. You must have a strong mind as well. Patience and perseverance. And one more thing, go steady, step by step. No need to show the zeal of a runner vying for a gold medal. We must respect the mountain we are climbing. Don't ever think that you are going to conquer the mountain. Remember, if you show arrogance, you will be invoking the wrath the mountain. We humans cannot survive the fury of the nature.'

David had said these words to an Aussie who had given up the hike halfway through. In the beginning, that pretentious man had a smug smile on his face and was always in the vanguard, showing off his muscles, cracking jokes, dancing and singing to impress the team, especially the women. He behaved as though he was sure he would be the first one to land at the summit. But by the time they reached Horombo Hut, he ran out of steam. Sleepless and breathless, he had an unbearable headache and vomited vehemently. He got cold feet at the sight of the mountain and finally did a vanishing act before everyone else woke up next the morning. But strangely, the couple from Denmark who were in their sixties, had successfully covered the distance so far, continuing confidently with a slow and steady pace.

By the time they reached Gilman's Point, oxygen levels had dipped drastically. Many more hikers walked past Mohanaswamy. As he trudged upward through the frigid air, Mohanaswamy's body began giving up. Once or twice he even toyed with the idea of going back, but decided against it. No, I will not give up. And yet, it makes no difference in whichever direction I go, backwards or forward. If I go back there will be no one waiting for me. And even if I go forward, there will be no one for me. But keeping the foot forward makes some sense at least. I have already embarked on this journey. If I finish it successfully, I can be happy with the thought that I did not accept defeat. I have suffered enough defeats in life. I don't want one more.

Gilman's Point is said to have received its name after a mountaineer called Gilman,who was the first to scale it. Overjoyed by his success, he declared that it was the topmost point of Kilimanjaro. However, his joy was short-lived as another hiker proved that Uhru Peak was the topmost peak. So far we have believed in it, but something else may come up in the future and belie our notion. We don't know what the future has in store for anyone, Mohanaswamy mused.

At Gilman's Point, Mohanaswamy insisted that he would lie down and take rest for ten minutes. But David did not concede. 'Better not, my child. Lying down will only make matters worse. You shouldn't sleep at such high altitude. Due to low oxygen you may die in your sleep. Keep walking, we have almost reached Uhru Peak. Now it's just a matter of two to three hours, that's all. Look there, the eastern horizon is already crimson,' he said, pointing to the sky.

'You are worried that I may die, right? Well, I am not scared of death, David. But I must sleep right now,' Mohanaswamy insisted and lied down on the rim of a rock, trying to nap. But soon he experienced a chilly fear rising from his navel and spreading through his body. Will this be the last time I sleep? It will be impossible for David to carry my body down. So he will probably push my body off the mountain and quietly walk down home. What will my friends and acquaintances think of me if they hear the news? Will they smirk at my defeat? Will they make fun of me?

Mohanaswamy's chest felt tighter. He instantly ran out of breath, breaking out in cold sweat. His heart raced fast as though it would blast. Death is cruel. The very thought of it is nerve-raking. He stood up. 'Come on, David, let's keep moving,' Mohanaswamy asserted, taking the lead this time. David simply smiled, he had seen many such people over the years. One must take off all masks in this difficult terrain of Kilimanjaro, one must steer clear of all ego, it is only then that the mountain will embrace them with open arms.

And finally, they made it to the summit.

Yes, they were there, at the summit, feeling on top of the world. The crowd erupted with whoops and cheers of excitement, relieved to be standing and breathing at Africa's highest point, after a long and strenuous journey.

The sun beamed through the sky, spreading light everywhere and warming their spirits. Now, no more torturous climbing. No more exertion. No more worries. Mohanaswamy felt as if he had just escaped from the jaws of death. A signboard read: 'You are now at the Uhru Peak, the highest point in Africa'. David leapt towards the board and standing there he frantically waved to Mohanaswamy, 'Come on, hurry up!'

A teary-eyed Mohanaswamy walked slowly, dragging his feet. On approaching the summit he couldn't control his emotions. He hugged David and broke down. He sank and wept out loud, unmindful of the presence of so many strangers. David felt sorry for him, he was used to seeing people celebrating at the peak, not crying. Climbers hugged one another in jubilation, posing for photos in the backdrop of the alpine scenery. But this sadness was unusual. David caressed Mohanaswamy's back. Mohanaswamy's grief was compounded by the affectionate touch. For how many more days will I conceal this fire inside me, Kilimanjaro? I have no capacity to hold it back like you. You are a huge mountain. I am a mere mortal. I don't want this pain, I don't want this humiliation. I cannot keep these feelings bottled up, I just cannot ... Mohanaswamy sobbed as his own words and thoughts tormented him.

'Why are you crying like this, my child? It is not good for your health.'

'I am tired, David, I'm fed up. Tell me how long can I face this world alone? I am tired of putting up a lone fight.'

'Don't be scared of anything, my child. If you fear life, you will be miserable. You may have had a larger share of woes in life but you must bring forth the capacity to absorb everything. You must have the patience and believe that better days are ahead. Happiness and grief are mere illusions. Nothing stays on, nothing is permanent.'

'They say happiness will be enhanced when it is shared and similarly, grief will subside. But what should I do when there is no one whom I can call my own? With whom shall I share my emotions?'

'Tell me, who is our own and who is not? If we lay down strict rules for ourselves, we will end up feeling lonely. Sometimes those we meet during our journey can be our own. Now, stop crying. I will take you to a spectacular view.'

Wiping his tears, Mohanaswamy followed David who took him to the edge of a cliff. The vast plains stretched as far as the eyes could see, plains with their sandy soils and snowy layers. It was paradise. It was as if he was seeing the opulent, cosmic form of god. Mohanaswamy was awestruck. 'God, you are impossible to view because of your limitless form. My vision is too feeble to behold this vast, unalloyed beauty. You are the universe and I am a mere creature in it. Having seen these infinite and formidable landscapes, I can no longer be egoistic, I can no longer be vainglorious. You are my saviour. I will never ever question your existence. Now I realize none of my woes are big enough to brood over. None of my achievements are big enough to boast about. My struggles may at the most bring a smile to your lips. I am a mere particle of your breath!' he said feverishly, overcome with his emotions.

~

At the Marangu Gate, the main entry point to Kilimajaro, the trekkers' cheers rose to the sky. Happy and proud to have made it to the summit, they all had come back to the same point from where they had begun their momentous journey exactly six days ago.

Descending the mountain was not as laborious as ascending. It had taken five days to go up but just two days to come down. Increasing oxygen levels invigorated the trekkers as they went down the hill, headache, vomiting, fatigue – all gone. Breathing became easy again. There was renewed vigour, a new lease of life. As the temperature increased, people took off their layers of warm clothing, one by one. They had been drained of physical energy – but looked bright and breezy, waving encouragingly to other groups of hikers on their upward journey. 'It's great! It's a cakewalk! It's a breeze! Very easy! Go ahead! Hakunamatata! Kilimanjaro is heaven!' they screamed out in excitement. An Indian in a group was elated to see Mohanaswamy. 'How was it? Did you make it to the top?' he asked.

'Yes, I did. It was a fantastic experience!' Mohanaswamy said, beaming with pride.

'Will you ever come here again?' he asked.

'Certainly, why not?' Mohanaswamy said, giving him a thumbs up.

On receiving their climbing certificates, the Italian couple hugged each other tightly. They opened a champagne bottle as the crowd cheered in euphoria. Everyone joined in the celebrations with certificates in their hands. The elderly couple from Denmark couldn't believe their own success. They shed tears of joy for having gone through one of the most amazing experiences of their life. The boy from England was seen talking to his parents on his mobile phone. The young couple from the US were seen dancing. A woman trekker from Moscow treated everyone to ice cream.

Mohanaswamy sat in a corner savouring the tasty ice cream. David walked towards Mohanaswamy holding his certificate in hand. 'Do you believe in god, my child?' he asked.

Mohanaswamy was perplexed at the sudden question from David. 'Why do you ask, David?'

'It was a perilous climb fraught with danger. But god has brought you back safely. Say thanks to him and accept this certificate.'

Mohanaswamy was in a fix. His rational mind, which

was now restored to its original state with the availability of plenty of oxygen in the air, refused to shift its ground. After all, he did not believe in anything that could not be proved scientifically.

'No David, I don't believe in god. The thought of god comes to me only in some moments of weakness.'

'Okay then, no problem. But do you at least believe in our Kilimanjaro Mountain?'

'Yes, why not?'

'Then say thanks to Kilimanjaro and accept this certificate.'

'Thanks Kilimanjaro!' said Mohanaswamy, his eyes closed, as he took the certificate from David and shook his hand.

Standing still at a distance, the fire inside Mount Kilimanjaro's belly bubbled slowly.

P.S.

Insights
Interviews
& More...

'Mohanaswamy was my rebirth': In Conversation with Vasudhendra

Rashmi Terdal

When Vasudhendra published *Mohanaswamy* (2013), the first collection of gay short stories in Kannada, it created a stir in the literary world. The book came as a cultural shock to many, not only for its subject but also because it revealed the sexual identity of the writer. By then, Vasudhendra had established himself as a popular writer. His earlier works of fiction and non-fiction generally revolved around issues such as globalization and cultural crises, the socio-economic changes the IT industry brought about in the lives of middle class Brahmins and so on. While queer fiction in English has picked up in India in the recent decades, there is relatively less noise about it in regional languages, especially in Kannada. Being a pioneer of gay literature in Kannada, Vasudhendra says he spent sleepless nights fearing law and society after he released the book. In this interview, Vasudhendra talks about his journey as a writer, gender issues in society and literature, the challenges of coming out of the closet, and the confidence and sense of freedom he has been experiencing thereafter.

Rashmi Terdal: You had been working as a software engineer for many years. How did writing come about and what made you quit the high-paying job and take up writing full-time?

Vasudhendra: My writing was perhaps the result of my feeling of loneliness and insecurity. I started writing when I was two years into my job, sometime in 1996. I did not like the rat race in the corporate world though it meant a lot of money and comforts. I wasn't happy. I was feeling lost as my friends and colleagues were getting married one by one and settling down in life. The horror of the emptiness inside me and the worries about future prompted me to take refuge in writing. I began getting up early in the mornings to write for two hours before going to work. In about two months, I finished my first story collection, *Maneeshe*.

However, getting it published was a struggle. I had to pay a publisher to print the book. Hardly any copies were sold. Then I went to England as per the demands of my job. The four years in England were one of the creative best. I wrote *Yugadi*, a short story collection, a couple of essay collections and *Mithuna*, a translation of Telugu short stories. After coming back to Bangalore, I was keen on publishing my books but again, no publisher came forward. A journalist friend encouraged me to publish the books on my own. That is how my publishing house, Chanda Pustaka, was born. The response from readers was overwhelming. Then there was no looking back. A few years on, I gave up my career as a software engineer as I was confident of earning a living through writing. Soon I began publishing books by young Kannada writers besides my own books.

Mohanaswamy **introduced the gay world to Kannada literature. What made you take up the subject?**

I was struggling to come out of the closet and found literature the only means to reveal my identity to the world. Though I had begun to understand the language of my body at the age of thirteen, I suffered silently for nearly three decades for the lack of courage to declare it. Finally it became a question of life and death. The British writer E.M. Forster too went through such pain. His novel dealing with gay issues was not published until after his death. I did not want the world to know the truth about me after my death. That was how *Mohanaswamy* was born.

'Kaggantu' ('The Gordian Knot' in this series) was the first story I wrote with Mohanaswamy as the central character, sometime in 2009. It appeared under a pseudonym in a literary magazine. Many readers expressed their liking for the story through letters to the editor. I wrote more gay stories in quick succession and decided to publish them. Some of my friends discouraged me, saying that I risked losing readership. I went ahead despite that and brought out *Mohanaswamy* under my own name.

And how did your readers receive the book?

There was a mixed response. It did not go down well with a section of readers. The same readers who had liked my first gay story published under a pseudonym did not react when they came to know that the author was me. Critics were silent and the initial response of Kannada media was dull, while some English newspapers wrote about it. However, women readers and bloggers were more forthcoming in expressing their opinion. There were discussions about the book on social media. Gradually, the readers and the media opened up. My interviews began appearing in newspapers and TV channels. And once the book gained popularity, it went into three reprints in no time.

What surprised me was the response from the gay community in Karnataka. Young gays started approaching me, narrating their life stories. Nobody had written about them so far. While English-speaking gays in metro cities are exposed to homosexual literature, those living in smaller towns and villages do not have the advantage. Some called me up, some wrote to me and some met me personally. Many worried mothers also approached me, saying that they had found similar traits in their sons. I empathized and counselled them – I am a trained counsellor and that skill helped me immensely to listen to them. Some young gays told me that I was the first person in whom they confided about their sexual identity. So there I was, reaching out to people of the gay community and becoming their voice in a way.

Who was the first person in your family whom you confided in? What was the reaction of your friends and acquaintances?

I confided in my elder sister. I was over forty at the time. I was extremely tensed before approaching her. I did not know how she would take it. But thankfully, she was cool and receptive. 'Why did you disclose it so late? You should have told us long before,' she said. Her kind response came as a big relief to me. I felt liberated. It was a load off my mind and heart. I regained confidence in life. However, I still nurse a regret. My parents had passed away by then. I feel I should have revealed the truth to them when they were alive. They use to pressure me to get married, but I kept postponing it on one pretext or the other. I should have told them the reason. They loved me a lot, so I am sure they would have accepted me even after coming to know my true identity. I wouldn't have had to live a pretentious life all along.

Mohanaswamy helped me in disclosing the truth to the larger world – my friends, acquaintances and readers. They accepted me and continued to shower the same love on me as before.

Coming out is most important and also is a must. Every gay person must discuss it with their family members as early as possible in life instead of wallowing in fear, guilt and self-pity. It may take some time for the family to digest the fact, but ultimately they will embrace the truth. According to me, your family also has the right to know who you are. Society appreciates honesty and integrity. In fact, our society is far more liberal and advanced than our law.

Did you not fear the law when you released *Mohanaswamy*?

The Delhi High Court, in 2009, decriminalized homosexuality between consenting adults, bringing much hope to the LGBTQ community. It was only after that I mustered my courage to bring out *Mohanaswamy*. Then the unimaginable happened. On the book release day, on 11 December 2013, the verdict of the Supreme Court came out. The SC had upheld Section 377 of the Indian Penal Code that criminalized homosexuality, overturning the previous judgement of the Delhi High Court and leaving the matter of amending or repealing the Act to the Parliament.

It was a crazy, painful coincidence. I lost my mind after releasing the book. I spent sleepless nights worrying about the consequences. I ran to some lawyer friends. However, they told me not to worry much. It took a few months for me to come out of the anxiety. But the efforts were worthwhile. I must say *Mohanaswamy* was my rebirth. I am not leading a pseudo life any more. I am being honest to myself and to the society.

Certain religious leaders are openly opposed to homosexuality. According to them, the 'tendency' is something against nature, it is like a bad addiction. Some even offer a 'cure' for homosexuality through yoga and naturopathy. What is your take on this?

Who are they to decide that homosexuality is against nature? It is not a disorder that there exists a cure for it. I can only laugh at such biased, ill-informed views. When a man is attracted towards a woman or when a woman chooses to have sex with a man, it is considered natural. But if physical attraction develops between two same-sex people, how does it become unnatural? How can you call it an acquired habit? Who has given the right to people to pass such judgements?

Some of my acquaintances, on coming to know that I am gay, said, 'Well, we respect your choice'. What I want to tell such people is that don't call homosexuality a choice. It is not something related to lifestyle. It is natural to a person.

Historical and religious literary evidence indicates that homosexuality has been prevalent in India since ages. Ironically, the Indian government is still clinging to the laws made by the British for us way back in 1861, whereas, in Britain, homosexuality has been already decriminalized. LGBTQ rights in the United Kingdom have evolved remarkably over time and the community enjoys one of the highest degrees of liberty in the world. It is high time India repealed Section 377 of IPC and decriminalized homosexuality. There should be provision for homosexuals to get married and have children through surrogacy. In fact, the civil society in India has become much more modern in recent years and is way ahead of its law. Now our law must follow our society.

Even as we talk about surrogacy, we hear the news that the Union government has cleared the Surrogacy Regulation Bill, proposing a complete ban on the rent-a-womb trade, barring single persons and homosexuals from opting for surrogacy. What do you have to say about it?

It is a very ugly decision. It comes as a big blow to homosexuals who want to live together and settle down with children. The government must relook into the decision.

Let's talk about the stories. 'Bed Bug' is a very poignant one in this collection. Did you ever know a person like Shankar, the protagonist of the story?

Yes. A boy like him was my childhood friend. I was very attached to him. He was killed by his own family members as he turned out to be a transgender. 'Bed Bug' though has elements of fiction in it. While gays have their own share of sorrows, the life of transgenders is even more difficult and complicated.

In an interview to *Outlook* magazine in August 2015, Arundhati Roy said that she doesn't believe that there are only two genders. She said gender is a spectrum. Do you agree with her?

I completely agree with her. In fact, in my opinion, gender is not only a spectrum, it is multi-dimensional. Nobody has the complete knowledge about it. As I said before, if you try to penetrate into the world of transgenders, you will find that their problems are completely different. Hardly anybody has written about them. We need to have more literature on the LGBTQ community as a whole and discussions on the socio-legal issues affecting them.

You are the first writer in Kannada to write exclusively about homosexuality. Have other writers touched upon this issue before in the history of Kannada literature?

In Kannada literature, some writers have made references to homosexuality but not with a healthy outlook. Most of them perceive gay love as something which is frightening, ridden with guilt, done under inevitable circumstances and against nature. A case in point is the Jnanpith award-winning 1968 epic novel *Mookajjiya Kanasugalu* (*Dreams of Silent Granny*) by K. Shivaram Karanth. The wise old woman in this novel views a physical relationship between man and woman as holy. However, she considers lovemaking between two men vile and disgusting, and concludes that it is a behaviour that needs to be corrected. The depiction of gays is even worse in *Kuduremotte* (*Egg of a Horse*), a 1971 Kannada Sahitya Academy Book Prize-winning novel by Kamaroopi.

A degenerate character in this novel is gay and on him, the novelist has imposed all wickedness and perversion, portraying homosexuals in a highly prejudiced light. We can see similar homophobia in 'Bettadache' ('Beyond the Mountain'), a short story by Kum Veerabhadrappa, published in 1995. In his 1980 short story titled 'Beega mattu Beegada kai' ('Lock and Key'), author Yeshwant Chittal pities the protagonist because of his inability to be physically attracted towards women. The writer goes on to the extent of suggesting that death is the only solution for this 'abnormality'. Then, another short story 'Angla Nauka Captain' ('English Captain'), written in the 1950s comes to mind. Its writer, Masti Venkatesh Iyengar, 'forgives' the gay character for his 'folly' committed due to non-availability of women. In U.R. Ananthamurthy's story 'Clip Joint' (1964), there is a mention of homosexuality. Stuart, a character in the story says that he was gay when he studied in a public school in London. But later when he joined university, he found a 'solution' to this problem in the company of women. These are wrong conceptions about homosexuality.

However, things have changed for the better in the recent past. Contemporary writers like Mitra Venkat Raj, M.R. Dattatri, Guruprakash Kaginele, Sudesh Shetty, Chidananda Sali, Nagraj Vastare, and K.V. Akshara have attempted to portray gays in their fiction with a humane touch. However, sometimes, when writers other than gays portray homosexual characters, we can see that it is more out of sympathy, curiosity and the need to bring in diversity. There should be more attempts to give a larger picture of the lives of the homosexual communities.

August 2016

Your Arrival is My Right

Vasudhendra

My eyes are full of sleep, and my heart is parched,
Let dreams rain in cold showers to quench my thirst.

The ground is ready, so are the limbs of my aching body,
Come, my dear beloved, draw me a supple rangoli –

Let the colours merge, yours and mine, to make a flower,
Let butterflies be drawn to it and marvel at its power,

Let the flower bloom and spread its fragrance,
Let butterflies hover over it and witness the grace.

If the wind blows, let it leave the flower of our colour alone,
This is your grand art; let me be the instrument of your goal.

My eyes are full of sleep tonight, and my heart is parched,
My wait is like Shabari's, and my body is the berry orchard.

Let dreams rain in cold showers to quench my thirst,
You are late tonight, my beloved, your arrival is my right.

I wait for your pleasure, beloved, whenever you have time.
I am now tempered steel, come, shape me the way you want.

I do not wish the world, just this much:
I want to sleep tonight like soaked earth.

And when I wake up in the middle of the night,
Dear beloved of mine, I want you to hold me tight.

This night will pass, with or without you, and tomorrow,
Let us merge our colours to make another rangoli for you

Let not the malice of the world touch us,
Until tomorrow, until I am born in you.

(Translated from the Kannada by Shashikumar and Dibyajyoti Sarma)

ನಿನ್ನಾಗಮನವೀಗ ಎನ್ನ ಹಕ್ಕು

ಕಣ್ಣ ತುಂಬ ನಿದ್ದೆ, ಮನವೆಲ್ಲಾ ಒದ್ದೆ
ತಣ್ಣಗೆ ಬರಲಿ ಕನಸು, ಒಣಗಿಸದಿರಲಿ ಮನಸು

ಸಂಗಾತಿ ದೊರಕಿದ ಬಳಿಕ, ರಂಗೋಲಿ ಅರಳದೇನೋ ಸಖ?
ಅಂಗಳವಿದೋ ಸಿದ್ಧ, ಅಂಗಾಂಗಗಳೂ ನಿನಗೆಂದೇ ಬದ್ಧ

ಚಿಕ್ಕೆಗಳು ಕೂಡಿ ಹೂವಾಗಲಿ, ಚಿಟ್ಟೆಯೂ ಹಾರಿ ಬಂದು ಬೆಪ್ಪಾಗಲಿ
ಚಿಕ್ಕೆಗಳೊಮ್ಮೆ ನಕ್ಕು ಆಗಸದಿ ಮರೆಯಾಗಲಿ, ಚಿಟ್ಟೆಯ ದೀಪ ಕಂದದಿರಲಿ

ಜೋರಾಗಿ ಬೀಸಿದರೂ ಗಾಳಿ, ನೆಲದ ತಂಪು ಚಿತ್ರವ ಹಿಡಿದಿಡಲಿ
ಬೇರಾವ ನಿಯಮಗಳೂ ಎನಗಿಲ್ಲ, ಚಿಕ್ಕೆಯೂ ನಿನ್ನದು ಚಿತ್ರವೂ ನಿನ್ನದು

ಶಬರಿಯೂ ನಾಚುವಂತೆ ಕಾದವನು ನಾನು, ನಿನ್ನ ಹಣ್ಣನು ಕೊಳೆಯದಂತೆ ಕಾಪಾಡಿದವನು
ನೀ ಬರುವುದೀಗ ನಿನ್ನ ಕರುಣೆಯಲ್ಲ, ನಿನ್ನಾಗಮನವೀಗ ಎನ್ನ ಹಕ್ಕು

ಕಾಯಿಸಿದೆ ನೀನೆಂದು ಬೇಸರವೆನಗಿಲ್ಲ, ಯಾವ ಕಹಿಯೂ ಈಗ ನನ್ನೊಳಗಿಲ್ಲ
ಕಾಯಿಸಿದ ಲೋಹ ನಾನೀಗ, ನವ ಎರಕಕೆ ಸಿದ್ಧವಾಗಿಹ ಜೀವ

ಸಿಕ್ಕಾಪಟ್ಟೆ ಬಯಕೆಗಳು ಎನಗಿಲ್ಲ, ಚಿಕ್ಕ ಪುಟ್ಟ ಸಂಗತಿಗಳೇ ಎಲ್ಲಾ
ಫಕ್ಕನೆ ನಡುರಾತ್ರಿ ಎಚ್ಚರವಾದಾಗ, ಪಕ್ಕದಲಿ ನೀನಿರಬೇಕು ಗೆಳೆಯ

ಗೊತ್ತೆನಗೆ ಇಲ್ಲಿ ಯಾವುದೂ ಶಾಶ್ವತವಲ್ಲ, ಬಿಟ್ಟು ಕೊಡುವೆ ಮನವ ಹೊಸ ರಂಗೋಲಿಗೆ ನಾಳೆ
ಕೆಟ್ಟ ಜನರ ಪಾದ ಆ ತನಕ ಮನವ ಮೆಟ್ಟದಿರಲಿ, ಹುಟ್ಟಬೇಕಿದೆ ನಾನು ಮತ್ತೊಮ್ಮೆ ನಿನ್ನ ಗರ್ಭದಲಿ

(Kannada original for 'Your Arrival is My Right')

Harper Perennial presents special editions of its finest books in translation

Age of Frenzy
Mahabaleshwar Sail
Translated from the Konkani by Vidya Pai

A Life Incomplete
Nanak Singh
Translated from the Punjabi by Navdeep Suri

Mohanaswamy
Vasudhendra
Translated from the Kannada by Rashmi Terdal

The Music of Solitude
Krishna Sobti
Translated from the Hindi by Vasudha Dalmia

No Presents Please: Mumbai Stories
Jayant Kaikini
Translated from the Kannada by Tejaswini Niranjana

A Preface to Man
Subhash Chandran
Translated from the Malayalam by Fathima E.V.

The Secret Garland
Andal
Translated from the Tamil by Archana Venkatesan

Shala
Milind Bokil
Translated from the Marathi by Vikrant Pande

The Weary Generations
Abdullah Hussein
Translated from the Urdu by the author

Written in Tears
Arupa Patangia Kalita
Translated from the Assamese by Ranjita Biswas

Bhima: Lone Warrior
M.T. Vasudevan Nair
Translated from the Malayalam by Gita Krishnankutty

Chemmeen
Thakazhi Sivasankara Pillai
Translated from the Malayalam by Anita Nair

Ghachar Ghochar
Vivek Shanbhag
Translated from the Kannada by Srinath Perur

Hindutva or Hind Swaraj
U.R. Ananthamurthy
Translated from the Kannada by Keerti Ramachandra & Vivek Shanbhag

The Liberation of Sita
Volga
Translated from the Telugu by T. Vijay Kumar & C. Vijayasree

A Life Misspent
Suryakant Tripathi Nirala
Translated from the Hindi by Satti Khanna

The Sea Lies Ahead
Intizar Husain
Translated from the Urdu by Rakhshanda Jalil

Selected Poems
Joy Goswami
Translated from the Bengali by Sampurna Chattarji

Wild Animals Prohibited: Stories/Anti-stories
Subimal Misra
Translated from the Bengali by V. Ramaswamy

Wild Words: Four Tamil Poets
Malathi Maithri, Salma, Kutti Revathi and Sukirtharani
Translated from the Tamil by Lakshmi Holmström